A
SHOOT

A SHOOT

Blood Red Turns Dollar Green Volume 2

PAUL O'BRIEN

Skyhorse Publishing

Skyhorse Publishing books may be purchased in bulk at special discounts for sales promotion, corporate gifts, fund-raising, or educational purposes. Special editions can also be created to specifications. For details, contact the Special Sales Department, Skyhorse Publishing, 307 West 36th Street, 11th Floor, New York, NY 10018 or info@skyhorsepublishing.com.
Skyhorse® and Skyhorse Publishing® are registered trademarks of Skyhorse Publishing, Inc.®, a Delaware corporation.

Visit our website at www.skyhorsepublishing.com.

10 9 8 7 6 5 4 3 2 1

Library of Congress Cataloging-in-Publication Data is available on file.

Cover design by Owen Corrigan

ISBN: 978-1-5107-0934-8
Ebook ISBN: 978-1-5107-0937-9

Printed in the United States of America

CHAPTER ONE

October 9, 1972.
Three days after Annie's murder.
New York.

Danno Garland had no reason left to be alive. When he heard what happened to his wife, he wanted to follow her—when he identified her body, when he got home and lay on their bed alone. He especially wanted to die when he realized that he had put her in that position in the first place. He *wanted* to follow his wife. But he couldn't. Not until he made right her death. And if everyone in the wrestling business had to lose so he could do that, then so be it. His mind was made up and he was going to see this thing to end, no matter the cost. Beginning immediately.

The car bounced, at odds with the weather-worn dirt track. Wet branches rubbed and slapped the metal of the car as it eased through the tight wooded passage until they came to a clearing. In the distance, the shining headlights of a ring of parked cars formed an illuminated circle. Apart from the secretly invited, there was nobody around for miles. Just hills, forests, and darkness around the edges.

Upstate New York was a perfect place for Danno to start his journey toward his wife.

Ricky Plick's concerned eyes checked on his boss in the rear-view mirror. He watched Danno look out his window as they approached the waiting cars. Ricky hoped for a sign to turn around—something to tell him that Danno wasn't going to go through with it. Both men had just come back from Texas, where they had been brought to a small white waiting room. Ricky hung back while Danno was escorted down the hallway to gently touch his wife's cold face; he had made noises that only the truly heartbroken make. Ricky knew his boss wasn't going to tell him to turn around.

They pulled into the last remaining gap and added their headlights to the ring of blinding light. Even with his wipers off and the rain walloping the windshield unmercifully, Ricky could still make out the open grave at the center of the lights.

"Let's get out of here, boss," Ricky said calmly. "We can take our time to rethink this."

Ricky knew that Danno was a cerebral man. A man hardwired for strategy over rash decisions. It was that very trait that had kept Danno at the top of their business for the last few years. Maybe Ricky could still appeal to that side of Danno.

"Boss?"

"I'm not going anywhere," Danno replied simply as he watched a man get pulled from the car directly ahead.

The captive man's face was covered and his hands were tied behind his back. He fought a little but not like a man who believed he could get away.

"He was with us when . . . it happened," Ricky said of the man who was now on his knees beside the grave.

"Does he seem scared to you?" Danno asked.

Ricky looked at the man's slightly bowed head and replied, "You don't need to do this."

"You can leave any time you want," Danno replied.

Ricky had watched Danno enter into the cutthroat wrestling business late in his life. He saw for himself how Danno was ignored and dismissed for years by the other bosses—the same bosses who were now parked in a halo beside him. Each car had a boss, and each boss represented a territory around the US with a professional wrestling company. Danno was New York and now the most powerful of them all. Not that he cared anymore. For him the wrestling business and all its secrecy and rules could go fuck itself. He had more important business to attend to.

The swirling wind and thick rain engulfed Danno as he opened his door and planted his foot in the soggy field. The cars of the other bosses started their engines. One by one, their cars reversed away from the grave and began their journey back to their hotels. The bosses showed their respect and unity by delivering the man Danno wanted. What Danno chose to do next, none of them wanted to see or be witness to, although they all knew exactly what the plan was.

Their hired hand, a washed-up former boxer called Mickey Jack Crisp, held the man in position on his knees.

"Danno," the man said from under the hood. "I know this is you. I had nothing to do with this. You won fair and square. You got my territory."

Danno gave the nod for Mickey to lift the hood. Underneath was Proctor King.

Proctor King had been the boss over the Florida territory. He and Danno had had a long, bitter, public dispute that had escalated to such a dangerous degree that it had brought threats to both their families. Their rivalry had ended only three nights before—with Danno outmaneuvering Proctor and taking over his territory. On finding out he had been flanked, Proctor had warned Danno that he would get retribution. That same night, Danno's wife was murdered in a small Texas hotel room.

"Jesus Christ, Danno. I didn't . . . I was with you. I didn't do anything," Proctor shouted.

Mickey put a .38 Special to Proctor's head and waited for the order. Proctor looked down and saw the pooling rain at the bottom of the grave in front of him. Ricky watched from the car.

"I didn't do it," Proctor said with his eyes firmly planted on Danno's.

"I told you that we were going to do this again someday," Danno said as took the .38 Special from Mickey Jack's hand and put it to Proctor's right eye. "You threatened my family once before and I put a gun to your face, but I didn't act."

"Danno," Proctor pleaded. He knew this wasn't like the other time. This time Danno was different—more sure of what he was going to do.

Ricky quickly opened the car door and tried to get to Danno to calm the situation. Proctor opened his mouth to speak but Danno pulled the trigger and pumped a single shot straight into Proctor's head. Danno watched the rain torpedo the blood running from Proctor's open skull as Proctor slumped lifelessly forward.

"Boss?" Ricky called. "Danno?"

Danno spat on Proctor's body and turned to Mickey Jack. "Get rid of this piece of shit."

Mickey Jack unfurled a plastic sheet and began his work of making Proctor disappear. He wanted to get out of there as soon as possible. The money was great, but Proctor had brought him into the wrestling business; Mickey Jack felt a little bad rolling him into a dark, sopping grave.

Ricky approached and put his arm around his stunned boss. "Let's get out of here."

Danno was frozen.

"Danno. We're going," Ricky said as he steered his boss toward the car.

"Now I want Curt Magee," Danno said as he shrugged Ricky off. He dropped the gun and walked back to his car.

"What do you want to do about this?" Mickey asked as he approached with a garbage bag. Danno and Ricky stopped. Mickey opened the bag. The World Heavyweight Championship belt was inside. Danno reached in and took it out. He looked at it briefly before tossing it into the grave. Danno made his own way back to the car.

"Not a word about this to anyone else. None of the other bosses can know what just happened," Ricky said.

Mickey Jack nodded.

"You took the shot, just like it was planned. We can't leave any trace of anything," Ricky said as he stooped and picked up Danno's discarded weapon before bundling it tightly in his jacket. He wasn't happy with how exposed Danno was. Years of keeping him tightly wrapped and squeaky clean—all gone with one bullet.

"Can you stay in town for another couple of days? I might need you," Ricky asked. "I'll know for certain after Mrs. Garland's funeral tomorrow. Meet me at the same place at six."

Waiting in New York another day would be no problem to Mickey Jack. The wrestling guys always paid well and most of the time he hardly had to do anything to earn it.

Ricky walked back to the car, but something made him stop. He turned and watched Mickey wrap the last of Proctor in the plastic.

"Wait," Ricky shouted.

Ricky went back, stepped over Proctor's waiting body at the edge of the grave, and dropped down into the hole to retrieve the championship belt. It was dirty and wet.

"A lot of history," Ricky said as he looked up at Mickey. "It doesn't deserve to be left here like this."

Mickey put out his hand and helped Ricky out of the grave. Ricky hid the belt behind his back as he came closer to his car, where Danno was a waiting passenger in the back.

As Danno watched Proctor get rolled into the hole, he knew he needed to mourn, but he couldn't yet. Because nobody knew better than he that there would be more death to come.

CHAPTER TWO

The same night.
Nevada.

The driver was being driven.

Lenny Long sat in the passenger seat of the family car. After driving in shifts for nearly three days straight, everyone in the car was pissed off, and the desert heat—even at night—really wasn't helping matters. The Long family had driven from Florida to Vegas to start their new life and had only begun dragging all their worldly belongings into their tiny motel room when its phone rang.

It was the call to Bree to start her new job.

"Where is it?" Luke asked from the backseat. Both he and his toddler brother James Henry were sick of the traveling and upheaval.

"Around the corner," Lenny lied.

"Is it?" Bree mouthed.

Lenny shrugged. Vegas wasn't one of his towns. He had spent the last few years driving Danno Garland and his wife, Annie, wherever they needed to go. They had never needed to go to Vegas.

"Do I make a right?" Bree asked as she anxiously navigated the sign-infested streets.

Lenny's eye was drawn to the tan lines on his wife's finger that played as a constant reminder of her missing wedding and engagement rings. He swore to himself once again that he would get her rings back, no matter what. In Lenny's mind, they couldn't get back on track as a couple until he corrected his horrible decision to use the rings as an IOU to Danno Garland.

"Right?" Bree asked again.

"I don't know about this," Lenny mumbled away from the children.

"About the right turn?" Bree asked.

"No, the job," Lenny replied.

Bree tapped the map on Lenny's lap to get him to focus. She had explained this to her husband a hundred times since she had been informed she got the position. "I'm just going to be dealing the cards. That's all."

"There's a reason they don't let women work in these places. Or didn't until now."

Bree gripped the steering wheel and talked herself out of another argument. Things hadn't been great between her and Lenny even before they moved their whole lives across the country. His job with Danno had meant that Lenny was gone for days, sometimes weeks at a time. It had nearly killed their marriage. This big shiny mess of a town was now their clean slate and Bree was doing her best not to dirty it.

"That's all they've asked you to do for now," Lenny said. "Deal cards, I mean."

"Just look for the Plaza," she said.

Lenny snapped the map open in front of his face. "We're looking for Main Street."

Bree took a deep breath, "I know that." She tried to read all the hundreds of signs as they rolled by.

Every now and then Luke would crane his neck and "whoa" at the pomp and cheap splendor of the buildings and their gimmicks. It looked like the town could have been designed by one of his seven-year-old friends. There were motel signs and restaurant signs and signs for shows and clubs and gas and coffee shops. Red signs, blue signs, round ones, and square ones. Signs to tell you that there were signs ahead.

"Turn here," Lenny said from behind the map.

"Here?"

"Yeah, here."

Bree began to think that maybe Lenny was pulling them around in circles on purpose. She knew he didn't want to leave New York. She knew he hadn't wanted to leave his job. She also knew he'd keep all that to himself.

"We should be coming up between First and Second Street," Lenny said. Bree guided the nose of their car around the corner and onto a packed street that was both beautiful and gaudy. Lights, bright colors, flags, and banners. There was a giant cowboy and a huge star perched on the side of a casino. Down at the end of the crammed, sparkling street, the Union Plaza stood above everything else. It was tall and unconventionally designed with a gaping foyer that sucked the road right in underneath itself.

"Fuck, is that it?" Lenny asked.

"Says so right on top," Bree excitedly answered as she pointed at the big red letters on the roof.

"And they're hiring ladies?" Lenny asked one last time.

Bree slowed down. "We could just go straight to my folks and stay there, Lenny."

"I wanna see Granpa," Luke said from the back.

Lenny shook his head. To him, Las Vegas was the lesser of two evils. He might have been out of work, he might have been a near-stranger to his kids, but Lenny was still the man of the Long house. At least that's what he was trying to be. He'd be damned if his wife would go to her folks looking for a place for them to stay. The motel was fine for now, and even though it made him nauseated, Bree's job was fine for now too.

Lenny put his hand on his wife's leg. She was beaming as the reflection of the hotel flicked across their windshield. She was happy. Her family were around her, she was getting to earn her own money, and she could work on things with her husband. For the first time in a couple of years Bree was starting to think that maybe they could make it as a family.

Ricky didn't want to make the call. That feeling had become familiar to him lately. He felt as though he spent most of his time doing things that were against his nature. But business was business, and it was his job to protect the wrestling business at all costs.

He had parked outside a grimy bar about sixty miles from where they had buried Proctor's body. It was dark and quiet and still pouring rain. Ricky stood in the phone booth on the street. He dialed and waited for a voice to pick up at the other end.

"Hello?" answered the voice.

"Gilbert?" Ricky asked.

"Who's this?"

Gilbert was Proctor's fuckup of a son.

"You know who it is. Where's Proctor?" Ricky asked.

"Ricky, I told you yesterday and the day before, I don't know where my old man is. My mother doesn't know either, so stop calling her too."

"Well, your old man has obviously jumped ship, Gilbert. If he couldn't take working for Danno then he should have been fucking man enough to say it. When you do see him, tell that weasel that I'm stripping him of the belt."

Gilbert tried to respond. "I—"

Ricky slammed the phone down and tried to manage his own disgust at what he had just done. He had already contacted the few wrestling media outlets that were left and spun the story that Proctor

King was on the run because he wasn't man enough to accept a rematch with the giant Babu.

Danno had made the decision that Proctor had to die. Now Ricky had to clean up the fallout.

Danno went through the routine of getting out of his drenched clothes. He stood and looked at his bed. Their bed. After all those years of marriage, getting into bed alone was strange. Danno stood paralyzed in the master bedroom of a big house that held nothing for him anymore.

Downstairs, Ricky was locking the doors and pulling the blinds for the night.

"You okay up there?" Ricky shouted.

Danno didn't answer.

Ricky listened some more before taking the silence to mean it was safe to proceed. He quietly walked down the hall and peered up the stairs to make sure Danno couldn't see what he was about to do. Ricky slid his hand into Danno's wet coat and quietly took out a bunch of keys. He removed one of the keys and placed the rest back where he found them.

Above Ricky, Danno sat on his bed in silence. The frailty and feeling of restriction slowly closed in on him. All the years he worked and schemed to get the big house and the wall full of money meant absolutely nothing. Danno was left an old man, companionless. In his head he harassed himself about the time he didn't talk to Annie for nearly a month because of something she said about his mother. He couldn't remember what. And the time he frightened her after that dinner party. How he let her rot for years on those pills. The time he told her he couldn't have children.

He thought of Proctor's head pressed against his gun. The startling whack of noise as he pulled the trigger. It made him sick. All this made him sick. Seeing Annie laid out on the metal table; knowing that her killer was still alive.

Danno got up and walked quickly to his bathroom, where he crouched to vomit in his toilet bowl. Just a few days ago, he was king. He managed to outmaneuver the other bosses not only to keep his New York territory, but to add San Francisco and Florida to his new empire. It all had to happen with precision. That's why he felt he had no choice but to agree with his wife when she suggested she go and negotiate for Texas.

Danno was the first boss in their business's history to move outside his own boundary lines and buy up other territories. That made him a huge threat to the other bosses. When was he coming for their patch? How long until he had the whole business to himself?

He thought about his celebration the night Annie was killed, everyone laughing and backslapping each other. He now knew that at the same time his wife had been lying on the floor of a small, dingy hotel room in Texas. Another thought to make him sick. Like the thought of having to kill again. The thought of never seeing her again. Danno slumped to the floor of his bathroom and looked out to their bedroom. Or his room, now. It looked like old people lived there. He remembered leaning into her cold ear and whispering, "I promise you I'll make this right before we meet again." The only comfort he allowed himself was the fleeting thought that maybe Annie was waiting for him. There was nothing else of meaning left. He was old and scared without her. The house was too big all of a sudden, and the noises outside were worrying. Every couple of minutes he'd have to check a window to make sure there was nothing unusual coming his way.

From the floor, Danno saw the leg of his carefully laid out suit on the end of the bed. He knew that beside it lay a single bullet waiting in the chamber of his chosen revolver. It was a bullet that had his name on it. When the man who killed his wife was dead, Danno would come back, put on that suit, and let that one bullet take him to meet his wife once again.

October 10, 1972.
Four days after Annie's murder.
New York.

For many years the NYPD's dysfunction was a private, dirty little secret. But now its corruption was so well known that Hollywood had even begun to make movies about it. It was an organization that was rotten from the top down: an old boy's club that made false arrests, fabricated evidence, and engaged in racketeering, beatings, bribery, and even attempted murder.

The NYPD was a festering wound down the middle of a dying city.

Nestor Chapman tapped lightly on the one door in the world he hated entering. Even before the new boss had showed up, Nestor hated that door.

"Come in," called the voice from inside.

Nestor turned the handle and walked sheepishly into the captain's office.

"Have a seat," Captain Miller said.

Near retirement, the captain reminded Nestor more of a doctor than a captain. He was long and lean and had a perfectly shiny bald head.

Nestor sat and tried to assess the situation. He had been in Miller's company a few times since Miller arrived from Brooklyn, but never on his own. He very much liked it that way.

"Did anyone ever tell Cooper that he types like a fucking retard?" the captain asked as he tried to make sense of a report on his desk.

Nestor smiled and nodded, in league with his boss. The captain closed his folder and focused on Nestor.

"Tell me what you know about Danno Garland," the captain said frankly.

Somewhere in his head Nestor had been waiting for that question, but when it came it still seemed foreign to him.

"Well," he began. "Not much. He's a promoter here in the city. Across the northeast here. Wrestling. Or professional wrestling.

Seems to have made some real money over the last few years judging by his . . . the way he lives now. I . . . I . . . he's . . . low to the ground. Doesn't cause trouble. I don't know."

Miller watched Nestor's face very carefully. He leaned back in his creaky chair and thought for a second before following up. "You've been following Troy Bartlett for a number of months," said the captain, making his words both a question and a statement.

Nestor nodded. He too leaned back and tried to make himself look less guilty of something.

"And this man, Troy Bartlett, is Danno Garland's lawyer?" the captain asked.

Nestor shrugged and adjusted his body some more.

"And Danno's name never comes up when you're digging around Bartlett?" Captain Miller asked.

"He does something for Garland but there's never been anything we could move in on. I'm interested in Bartlett for different matters. Missing monies. Shady practices. That kind of thing."

The captain again disconnected from the conversation to think. Nestor had heard how shrewd Miller was and how he played a tight game in terms of strategy. Such talents around this particular topic made Nestor anxious.

"Is there something . . . ?" Nestor let his sentence trail off. He wanted to know what this was about but didn't want to ask directly. He knew that a high-ranking officer wasn't fishing around for no reason.

Captain Miller leaned into his desk and looked Nestor straight in the face. "I've got a US senator who was stabbed in both legs a few blocks from here. I'm sure you've heard by now. It's everywhere. My goddamn wife has called me ten times today to tell me it's on the radio and the TV."

"Yeah, I heard. Hell of a thing," Nestor answered, trying to sound sympathetic.

"Yeah, well, the senator says he doesn't know what happened. He gets a lot of crazies, he says. Could have been anyone. He's calling for more money from the federal government for policing."

Nestor nodded accordingly. "This city is . . . everyone who goes out there is on their own," Nestor replied, sounding totally unaware of his responsibility.

"Well, we might have something to do with that. Don't you think?" the captain asked.

Nestor realized how stupid his answer was. He wanted to get the conversation back on track. "What makes you think Garland had anything to do with it?"

The captain stood up and walked to the mesh-covered window. "When the news broke, I personally got a call from the head of the Athletic Commission. He comes down here to our boxing club. Maybe you've seen him around. Melvin Pritchard? Anyway, he says that the senator, just before he was attacked, was scheduled to bring Garland before a committee on match fixing or some such nonsense."

"I didn't know that," Nestor said, lying.

Miller turned back from the window. "US Senators don't get stabbed on the street in the United States of America. Not even in this fucking city. I just need to know whether I should chase this wrestling guy or discount him and move on. 'Cause someone is gonna notice . . ."

The captain stopped himself.

There it was, Nestor thought. The reason he was called in at all. A high-ranking politician with a national profile gets knifed on the street and someone is either getting squashed for mishandling it or highly rewarded for fixing it. There had been talk around the department of the First and Fourth precincts being amalgamated under one roof. No police house in the whole of New York had *two* captains. Nestor thought that Miller was fixing to move up the chain.

"This police force can't afford another high profile fuckup," the captain said. "If they're going to make another movie about us . . . it's gotta be . . . we've . . . we're the good fucking guys, you understand?"

Nestor nodded in agreement. Captain Miller looked at his detective and couldn't decide on him one way or the other.

"I've ordered some officers to go out and shake a few bushes. Make a few inquiries into this Garland person."

Nestor nodded.

"Just so you know," the captain said.

"Okay," Nestor answered, not quite knowing what he should say.

The captain sat back down and lifted his pen, ready. "So you have nothing to tell me in this regard at this time?"

Nestor shook his head. "Not at this time," he said.

"But when you do . . ."

"But when I do . . ."

Nestor sat easy even though he felt like bursting out the door and running to his car. He knew he needed to stay ahead of new attention that was about to come from his own department.

Luckily, he had already started.

October 10, 1972.
Four days after Annie's murder.
New York.

Danno descended the large stairs, dressed in a black suit. He really tried to resist it but in the end he felt compelled to shout. "Hello?" He wasn't sure whether he wanted somebody to reply or not.

He picked up his phone and dialed Lenny Long from his pocket phone book. The number just returned a disconnected tone. Danno tried again but got the same result.

In the middle of everything, Danno had no idea where his driver had gone. The more days that went by without hearing from Lenny, the more Danno began to think something bad had happened to him too. That was the last thing that Danno wanted to even consider.

Even though Danno would never tell Lenny to his face, Danno considered him a friend. Or a son. Lenny could be reckless, naïve, and sometimes a little dumb—but Danno loved him.

Danno put his phone down, composed himself, and walked to the front door. He noticed a note lying on the floor. Its appearance heightened his anxiety again.

"Hello?"

He carefully walked toward it and checked the doorways of his hallway before he stooped.

He slowly opened it, and read:

THERE'S A HEATWAVE COMING UP FROM FLORIDA. YOU BETTER COVER UP.

He didn't recognize the handwriting, but the letterhead was something he had seen a thousand times before.

CHAPTER THREE

Ricky woke and gingerly put his right leg out of the bed first, trying to gauge the pain level before coaxing his much worse left leg to follow. Both actions sent a stabbing sensation to the base of his neck, which in turn rang as a squeal of pain in his ears.

Most retired wrestlers woke up the same way after years of taking bumps in the ring—cautiously. Knowing when you're going to be slammed, tossed, and dropped doesn't lessen the pain of *being* slammed, tossed, or dropped.

Pain or not, Ricky made sure not to make too much noise, because he didn't want to wake Ginny who was still asleep beside him.

He often prayed that there would never be an emergency at night; neither man would be able to get out of bed in time to survive. They both had long careers and were now paying the physical price.

Mornings were the worst.

He shuffled out of their bedroom and cracked various joints along the way. He softly closed the door between their bedroom and the kitchen. He fired up the radio and news came through the speakers: ". . . Mr. Tenenbaum left the hospital and was driven to an unknown location. Eyewitnesses recounted the senator's struggle in simply entering the waiting vehicle because of the dressing on both his legs."

Ricky quickly flicked the off button. Hearing the report sent a chill through his body, which further reaffirmed that that side of the business was something he wanted to stay many, many miles from.

Ricky was a wrestling man through and through. Had been all his life. He was Danno's number two—the Booker. He was responsible for making the matches and deciding the winners. It was his role to make the card new and exciting every time he entered a different town. Danno handled the office, contracts, and business, and Ricky handled everything once they were on the road.

Ricky dearly wished that they could get back to that, but he wasn't sure Danno was thinking the same way. Or that he ever would again. He knew that Danno's actions were leaving a usually clandestine business too exposed, too open. Ricky was going to need to work smart and try to cover all the bases that Danno was missing.

There was still the business to run. A business that fed on backroom deals and sleight of hand. And a card at Madison Square Garden.

Ginny stood at the sink of their small apartment. He wore a fresh white vest, and his short hair was washed and slicked back with a comb. His stubbled face was half covered in soap. Back in the day, Ginny used to shave with a blade, just like his father before him. Now he needed Ricky's help to get the right side of his face done.

Ever since his car got smashed off the highway, things had been tougher for Ginny. And Ricky.

"Don't leave the spot under my nose," Ginny said.

Ricky looked over his glasses and gently navigated his way around Ginny's face.

Ginny pointed impatiently. "There. Under my nose. There."

Ricky swirled the razor around in the water and tapped it twice off the side of the sink.

"I heard you," Ricky said.

Every day was the same. Ginny liked to be fresh faced. He just couldn't trust his own hand to stay steady anymore.

Ricky placed the razor on Ginny's neck and Ginny tilted his head in sync.

"The bit," Ginny said pointing under his nose.

"I'm going to slit your throat if you don't stop bothering me," Ricky warned.

Ginny grabbed the small mirror and checked under his nose as Ricky continued.

"You know, it would be easier to do this if you just stayed still," Ricky said.

Ginny burst into tears. Ricky stopped what he was doing but otherwise didn't even acknowledge it. The first few times Ginny cried like that after he came out of the hospital, Ricky begged Ginny to tell him what was wrong. Now, the tears just came and went. They were for nothing. They meant nothing. Neither man mentioned them anymore.

As soon as they came, Ginny wiped his tears, and they were gone. Ricky continued his morning job.

"Under my nose," Ginny said rubbing his eyes with his forearm.

Ricky also ignored Ginny's orders. The head trauma had left him repetitive, slower, more moody and emotional. He couldn't reach across his body and he suffered from debilitating headaches.

When it first happened, Ricky wanted his old Ginny back. Now he just accepted the way he was. After all their years together, and remembering how close he came to losing him, Ricky was just happy to have him any way he could.

"Why is there a gun hidden under our bed?" Ginny asked, perfectly lucid.

That was the way it went. Confusion to clarity. Neediness to independence. It changed hour to hour and minute to minute.

"You know what the city is like out there now," Ricky replied.

"It's wrapped up, though. Like you're trying to hide it."

"No," Ricky lied. "I got it for us. Do you want to leave your life in the hands of the cops we got?"

The morning light highlighted all of Ginny's scarring. The back of his head. Across his right shoulder, down the triceps, and around the forearm. He had already been too beat up to continue wrestling before he got rammed off the highway.

"I want us out," Ginny said as he flung the hand towel onto his shoulder and rubbed the side of his face dry.

"Out of what?" Ricky asked, knowing perfectly well what Ginny was talking about.

The phone on the wall in the kitchen began to ring. Ricky hurried, like an old person hurries, to answer the call. "Hello?"

"We got to meet up," the voice on the line said plainly.

Ricky immediately recognized who it was. "Okay," he answered.

"At the end of the bridge tonight at ten."

Ricky replied, "Can't. I've got to tape our matches for TV. How about four?"

"Is Danno going to be there?" the voice asked.

"I doubt it."

The caller hung up.

Nevada.

Lenny lay on the pink carpet of his motel room. James Henry silently watched his father intently from behind the prison bars of his crib.

"Do it," Lenny whispered without moving his lips.

"I don't want to," Luke answered anxiously from his standing position on the bed.

Lenny peeked with one eye and whispered, "You've laid me out, son. Now finish me."

Luke didn't really like wrestling anymore but he missed playing with his father. "I . . ."

"Big splash or elbow, son, this is your big finish. Listen to that crowd chant your name and you pick your spot," Lenny said as he reprised his role of prone wrestler.

Luke awkwardly half-jumped, half-fell and landed with a double knee drop right across his father's face. An angry and wounded noise escaped from Lenny as he rolled into the fetal position and cradled his own head in pain. It was so intense that he was afraid to breathe.

Luke stood and walked backwards until he felt the multi-colored bed at the back of his legs. He watched his father eventually draw in narrow, short, painful breaths. "Dad?"

Lenny rocked back and forth and moaned a little.

"I'm sorry," Luke said.

It felt like Lenny's jaw, nose, and skull were broken. "S'fine," was all he could release from his lungs.

Luke came closer and put a little hand on his father's shoulder. The younger son in the cot threw his bottle and clapped and gurgled at the show in front of him.

"You have to protect the people you work with," Lenny said and tapped his little boy's hand.

Luke cuddled into his father's back and whispered into his ear, "I don't like wrestling anymore."

Lenny wasn't sure which hurt more: the knees to the face or his son saying he didn't like wrestling. All he could do was lie there and try to refocus the vision back into his water-filled eyes. He could make out pea-green seats. Wood paneling. A wardrobe. Stacks of cash underneath the wardrobe.

What the fuck?

Luke nestled the top of his head into his father's neck and figured out a comfortable spot to snuggle.

"Bath time," Lenny said, shrugging him off. "Take your brother."

Luke tried to protest. "I don't want to . . ."

"Do it," Lenny ordered. "Fill up the tub and put your little brother in it."

"I don't know how. Mom does that," Luke argued.

"Get in there now and close the door."

Luke struggled to lift James Henry from the crib. He dragged his little brother's legs awkwardly over the top bar and strained to carry him. Lenny watched his kids make it across the room and then closed them in the bathroom. "Don't come out until you're both clean as a whistle."

Lenny stooped down to the money. He knew he had just found his wife's stash. The same stash she told him she didn't have anymore. The same stash she took from a bag that Lenny had been hiding in their garage. The same stash she had been going to use to leave Lenny with.

She took it from the bag in the garage because she thought it was Lenny's money she was taking—she thought it was theirs.

It wasn't.

The short journey fittingly took Lenny along Paradise Road. Bree was working the second day of her new job and Lenny knew he could get where he needed to be and back to the motel again before Bree got off her shift. He didn't tell her where he was going or, more importantly, *why* he was going there—because he made her a promise.

A promise he was now going to break.

A few hours before, Lenny had lain in his new, rock-hard motel bed and watched his wife sleeping. It was a small luxury that he hadn't had the time to enjoy much over the previous four years. He tried to look at her anew: her small ear lobes that got whiter when she was cold, the little cluster of freckles on her shoulder. He was reminded why he loved her. He hoped that she wasn't coming to the realization that she might have just settled for him.

He adored her and his boys.

But that didn't mean that he wasn't going to lie to them. Especially when it came to this.

He pulled onto the curb and eyed the little store on the other side of the busy Vegas street. "I'll be back in a second," he told his young sons as he cracked open his car door.

Luke panicked a little at being left on his own with his brother again. "Where are you going, Daddy?" Luke too could see clearly across the road and in his seven short years he had never had to wait in the car while his mother went into a store.

"I'll be a second. You wait here and look out for your little brother."

James Henry immediately reached out his arms for his father to pick him up. He was a lazy child who didn't speak much for a two-year-old. He just kinda sat there—cute, with clear skin and a blond, round, doughy head.

"He wants to go with you," Luke said, volunteering himself as translator.

"Just tell him I'll be a second. Can you do that?" Lenny replied.

"He's going to cry, Dad."

"No, he's not." Lenny got out, slammed his door closed and wiped the sweat of the desert from his brow.

James Henry immediately began to bawl. Lenny turned, saw his kid crying, and quickly turned away like he hadn't seen it. A crying child instantly stressed Lenny out.

What kind of man looks after the kids while the wife works?

He slowly looked back in the hopes that they were instantly asleep or something.

No such fucking luck.

Two little distressed faces looked at him from the dirty backseat window. "I just wanted to go to the store—right there—to get you both some candy," he shouted and mimed in an attempt to cross the road guilt-free.

It wasn't going to work. James Henry's bottom lip grew bigger with sorrow.

How does Bree calm them down?

Lenny remembered her saying something to him about cassettes one night after he came off the road.

"Do something, Dad," an equally flustered Luke shouted.

Lenny got back in the car and rummaged in the glove compartment.

"I just need two minutes to go there. Just two," Lenny said as he pulled out a few battered eight-tracks and turned on the ignition. He slipped a tape into the player. Soon a sweet a cappella children's song came through the speakers. Like magic, Lenny watched his youngest son's face turn from despair to curiosity.

"Mom," Luke joyfully pronounced.

Lenny felt a little dread run down his spine before he realized his boy was talking about Bree singing the song, and not out on the street somewhere watching Lenny trying to ditch their kids.

But his son was right, it was Bree. Singing a song for her kids in that beautiful voice that Lenny hadn't heard in a long time.

"I will get you something nice," he mouthed to no son in particular, as he slipped out of the car.

Luke watched as his father dodged the fast-moving traffic to get to the store. The boy desperately tried to see further but couldn't with his brother on his lap. He leaned over and rolled down the backseat window. He could hear the cars outside as they sped past.

The waiting was agony. Luke pushed James Henry off his legs, rose to his knees, and peeked slightly out the window. Lenny was still nowhere to be seen.

He peeked again.

James Henry was "singing" along with his mother and happily waving around his See 'n Say.

Luke thought his little brother would be fine in the car if he went and had a quick look in the store window. The older brother carefully opened his door and dropped his small foot onto the sticky

Vegas road. With the door open and blocking his view, he couldn't judge the oncoming traffic. He crouched down and watched the cars hurtling toward him.

On the back seat, James Henry was also crawling toward the open door. The sounds and the adventure his big brother was embarking on made him even more curious than his mother's song.

"Stay there, James Henry," Luke demanded, to no avail. "Do you hear me? Only I'm big enough," he said.

The baby propped himself up in a seated position in front of Luke and playfully threw his toy into the road. Luke turned and absent-mindedly followed the course of the toy.

"Luke," Lenny shouted as he stuffed a brown paper bag into his shirt on the other side of the road.

Luke froze with fear a foot into the road.

"Go back to the car," Lenny shouted. He knew by his son's face that he was shocked and confused, standing in the road. Lenny could also see a red Pontiac speeding closer to his child. He frantically tried to jostle with the oncoming traffic on his side of the road to make it to his boy.

"Luke, get back to the car now," Lenny ordered.

Luke didn't move. He couldn't.

Lenny yelled, "Run!"

The little boy just stood in place, totally helpless. The Pontiac wasn't slowing, and Luke wasn't moving. Lenny could also see James Henry turn himself around on the back seat and push his little legs outside the car in an effort to climb down onto the road. Lenny launched himself through the small, dangerous gaps in the traffic and snatched Luke up into his arms just as the red Pontiac sped past. He pushed his youngest boy further into the seat.

"I'm sorry, Daddy. I wanted to see where you went to," Luke said as he cried with fright on his father's shoulder.

"It's okay, little man," Lenny said as he gently bounced Luke up and down.

Lenny, Luke, and James Henry sat in the back of the Long family car listening to Bree sing them a lullaby as the craziness of Las Vegas rumbled outside their windows.

Lenny relived the stomach-churning events, cringing at the very narrow miss.

"What have you got in the bag, Daddy?" Luke asked through his flood of tears.

"Nothing, son," Lenny lied.

CHAPTER FOUR

New York.

Outside the church everyone was getting a little nervous about the floor-to-ceiling windows. People in the wrestling business liked to conduct their personal matters away from the gazing eye of civilians, and the clear church glass wasn't helping.

Wrestling money was all based on selling the personal rivalries and hatred that certain wrestlers felt for each other. Seeing them all together without violence would be damaging for the stories they were all trying to sell on their TV shows. The one thing the bosses of the territories wouldn't stand was their wrestlers breaking character or storyline in public.

The wrestlers on top of the card—those who could afford it—stayed in their blacked-out limos for fear of being seen socializing with their "sworn enemies." The lower-card wrestlers dispersed themselves around the grounds until the sermon began.

Ricky walked the pathway that was cut through the manicured gardens of the church grounds. The tree branches overhead leaned across each other to form a woven guard of honor. He knew it was going to be a long day. He had liked Annie and missed her terribly, too. Not that anyone was going to be thinking of him and his problems.

In Danno's absence, Ricky was unofficially appointed the Wrestlers' Wailing Wall. All disputes, matches, wrestling cards, and wrestler problems just fell to him by proxy. But Ricky had his own problems. He was focused on Ginny, alone and slightly confused-looking by the church door. Ricky wanted to put his arms around him and help him tuck in his ruffled shirt. He wanted to put his arms around him and protect him from what he had become: a joke to the younger wrestlers who took every opportunity to laugh at him when his back was turned.

Ricky could see the disrespect but he couldn't do anything to stop it. Like everything in the wrestling business, there was a facade that must be kept intact at all times. None of the Boys worked with fags. None of the Boys would shower with them or be seen with them. And the Boys certainly wouldn't take orders from one. So Ricky walked past his partner's smile and outstretched hand and marched straight into the church. For both their sakes.

On his way down the hard stone aisle he was grabbed gently by a well-pressed Texan. "The Garden is flat, Ricky," Wild Ted Berry said in a hushed tone.

Ricky nodded in acknowledgement. His silence didn't impress Ted one bit. "I'm telling you that the Garden is flat and all you can do is nod?"

Ricky nodded again and continued toward the top pew.

Danno's company was to tour around the Northeast and finish its loop once a month at the Garden. That was the New York company's stronghold. The building where they always gave a little more. A title match, a TV taping, a cage match—something extra. Something you didn't see at every card. Others expected a sold-out house, but Ricky was more realistic. The last time they ran a card in New York was only a couple of weeks ago—and they hadn't delivered their main event. It was the most hyped and anticipated main event in their history. The New York crowd rioted and tore up Shea Stadium. Not enough time had passed for them to forget. That's why the house was flat.

"Just a note of condolence for the boss," the Folsom Nightmare said before Ricky could build up a head of steam.

Ricky took the card. "I'll make sure he gets it."

"Terrible day."

Ricky again nodded and tried to move on.

"Doc says I'm good to go," Folsom said without real conviction. "My Achilles is healed all back up. Healed, get it?"

Ricky looked along the row and could see one of Folsom's many young sons trying valiantly to hide his father's crutch under the pew. Wrestlers who didn't wrestle didn't get paid, and there were a lot of young faces looking in Ricky's direction.

"Folsom . . ." Ricky began.

Folsom leaned in closer to talk about business. "I could start back in Battle Royals or something. The Boys will look out for me, Ricky. I could come over the top and take a bump on my back or something. I don't need to put pressure on my foot straightaway."

Ricky could see a proud father pleading with him in front of his family.

"We'll give it some more time," Ricky said as he lay a limp hand of comfort on Folsom's shoulder. "You'll be back soon."

Folsom forced a smile.

"You'd think Proctor King would have at least shown to pay his respects," Ricky said as he walked away with a heavy heart, knowing that the Folsom Nightmare, hurt in the ring, would never wrestle again.

He also knew that Proctor not being there would spread like wildfire.

Midgets, beauty queens, tattooed faces, gold sunglasses, new black suits, hugely obese twins, a bald old woman, toothless mountain men, islanders, a one-legged man, and a giant. Christ Church was stuffed with representatives from all over the wrestling world. All the other bosses from the National Wrestling Council were there. Even though their Annual General Meeting was officially off, promoters from Japan, Europe, and Africa still arrived. They all wanted to make sure that Danno saw them sad. If they could swing only one tour with Danno's huge champion, they could roll in the money. So they did what any self-respecting promoter would do—they out-cried each other.

"Where's the boss?" Ricky asked the huddled crowd at the top pew. Nobody knew.

Across the aisle, the chairman of the National Wrestling Council, Joe Lapine, wondered where Danno was too. Beside him stood the boss of the Carolinas, Tanner Blackwell.

"Danno killed his own champion," Tanner said to Joe.

"I tried for days to talk him out of it," Joe replied. "He was blind with rage."

None of the bosses ever cried when a world title got taken from someone, as it increased the chances that they were next in line to receive it.

"I heard he did it himself," Tanner said to Joe.

Joe leaned in and whispered, "What?"

"Last night. Danno did the job himself."

Joe shook his head disbelievingly. "No way."

Tanner smiled.

Hiring someone from outside to kill was one thing. The guy with the whole business in his hands doing the killing was something completely different.

"Not in a million years," Joe said.

Joe, like everyone else, didn't think Danno Garland had it in him to kill. But Tanner knew; he had paid to find out.

The priest shuffled from the sacristy door and his jowly face hung down like a melted candle. His entrance set a hush over the gathered mass. In this hush, most of the gathering daydreamed about *being* champion, *having* the champion, or about whoever it was holding them *back* from being champion. For those in the wrestling busi-ness, those three permutations of the one possession gnawed and prodded at them and demanded most of their time. With that heavyweight title came a lot of power and a lot of money. There wasn't a single person in attendance who didn't want both.

Ricky looked at Annie's casket and couldn't help but imagine what her last seconds were like. The cops wouldn't tell Danno much more than *where* she was found and *how* she was killed. They hadn't got to the *who* part yet. They said some prints were found and a man was seen walking toward her room.

"Please rise," the priest said from the altar.

Danno had been such an infrequent visitor that the priest never noticed that the husband of the deceased wasn't even in attendance.

Ricky noticed, though.

Outside, Danno stood with his back to the church wall and his face in the sun. He couldn't walk through the doors. His legs just wouldn't do it. He couldn't be close to her again until he fulfilled his promise.

"He's started," Ricky said from the large arched doorway in his most gentle voice.

"Did you find Curt Magee yet?" Danno said without looking away from the sky.

Ricky was uncomfortable with just how loose Danno was with his words in public. "I'm trying to keep things moving with the business. All the other bosses are in town and we have the Garden coming up."

Danno turned directly to his longtime confidante. "Fuck the business, Ricky. You find the man who killed my wife. You track him down and you fucking hold him till I get there. Do you hear me?"

Through the window Ricky could see everyone straining to look at them outside. Even the priest was distracted.

"Do you hear me?" Danno asked again, suddenly becoming overwhelmed. He stopped himself crying. "How can I go in there to her? How can I stand in the same room as her when I haven't made it right?"

"I'm sorry about what happened. My heart is broken for you, but ..."

"But what?"

Ricky walked a little closer and spoke a little softer. "Boss, you need to let yourself grieve or mourn or whatever it is people do at times like this."

Up close and on their own, Ricky could see just how broken Danno was. He was missing.

"I want him to feel like I do," Danno said.

"I know."

"No, you don't. I want the bastard to feel exactly like I did when I heard. Like I did when I had to see her laid out like that. I want his family to feel that loss. Like I am." Danno moved to leave. "And I will. If it's the last thing I do on this earth. I will make good on my promise. And I'll transfer this pain I have onto them."

Ricky struggled to verbalize his reluctance to follow his boss. Such words were unfamiliar to him, but Ricky was simply a retired wrestler—a man who loved the wrestling business. He wasn't a detective or hitman and, unlike a lot of the people at the ceremony, he had no desire to be.

Ricky followed Danno. "Where are you going?"

"If I have to ask for their help instead of yours, then I will," Danno said, meaning the other bosses. "I want Curt Magee found or I'm going to go like a tornado across all the territories until I find him."

Danno walked to the large gates as Ricky stopped in his tracks.

"'Cause someone out there knows where he is," Danno shouted back.

Ricky tried to figure out how to cool all this down. He knew that Danno accusing the other bosses of hiding a murderer wasn't going to end up good for Danno. Bosses couldn't just take each other out whenever they felt like it. That would make everyone at the top nervous.

In the wrestling business, funerals only grant you pity for a day. Then it's all about the money again. A weak and unfocused Danno was a gift to everyone who wanted what he had. And Ricky knew that everyone in that church was using the opportunity to gauge just how wounded Danno was.

Nevada.

Lenny felt stupid and childish and secretive—and excited. He simply didn't want word getting back to his wife that he was back looking at this sort of thing again. So a dingy, purple, public restroom it had to be.

He sat in the stall and quietly pulled out the brown bag from inside his shirt. Luke sat on the floor directly outside his father's stall with a mouth full of candy and his little brother on his lap, sucking on a popsicle. Their faces were a pleasurable, sugary mess and their fingers were too sticky to part.

Luke dropped one of his candy pieces on the restroom floor. He waited for his father's instruction to leave it where it fell. It never came, so he wiped the escaped treat and popped it in his mouth.

"You nearly finished in there, Dad?" Luke mumbled through his full mouth.

Lenny slipped a magazine from his paper bag and delicately opened it. He missed those glossy pages. The smell of a new publication. *USA Wrestling Chronicles.*

"Dad?" Luke asked again. "Are you nearly finished in there?"

A stranger entered and tried to figure out what two little boys were doing sitting on the floor of a public restroom. The seven-year-old's arm was still in one sleeve of his jacket, but the other empty sleeve ran underneath the stall where Lenny had his foot on it. Like holding a dog on a leash.

"Nearly finished, son," Lenny answered.

The bemused stranger went about his business.

Lenny hadn't been able to wait any longer to see if his debut as a referee made the magazines. Growing up in Long Island, Lenny used to buy stacks of those same magazines to catch up on all the matches and new champions in the wrestling world. He religiously tore out the center poster and replaced the image on his wall, based on who was new and cool. One man never got replaced on the Long wall, though—the Sugarstick, Shane Montrose.

Lenny considered the sneaking around his reconnaissance. After all, he'd have to know what was happening in the wrestling world if he were to go back. It was just a pity that wrestling magazines were always weeks behind. In the middle of Las Vegas, with his kids on the floor and his wife dealing cards, Lenny Long was the happiest man in the world. Because of wrestling.

It would soon make him feel a whole lot different.

New York.

The old back barroom was dark and smoky. Even the process of mourning had to be kept away from the public. Every major boss and their top wrestling stars were dotted along the chipped tables and cozy booths. When someone of note in the wrestling business died, it was a good opportunity to get your face out there. Make contacts. When someone belonging to a boss died—you better be there or your name got blackened. But when the wife of a boss got killed, and the killer was still out there, you better be there or theories started to form and questions began to get asked. And so Annie Garland's wake was standing room only.

The back room of a nightclub wasn't where Annie Garland should have been remembered, but rules are rules. Protect the business at all times. Even when business is the last thing on your mind.

Danno sat alone, in thought at the top of the room. Everyone was giving him space and time. He wasn't eating, he wasn't drinking. And he wasn't talking. Most of the other "mourners" were trying to figure out how long was respectful enough to stay sober. They were all together, on a day off, in a bar. That never happened. The temptation to capitalize on that perfect storm of circumstance was excruciating. Even with the bar signs covered over and the tables draped in flowers, it was still a shit-hole, and Danno knew it.

A bar like this would have been the last place a woman like his wife would go if she were alive.

Outside, the Sugarstick, Shane Montrose, late and hurried, marched down the dark alleyway toward the wake. As always, he was dressed in style. His suit was beige pinstripe with a single breast pocket and gold buttons with matching bell-bottoms. His shirt was blue and his tie was red silk with a paisley design. Shane Montrose was one of the biggest wrestlers of all time. Over his many years in the business he saw and did it all—nearly. That life was evident for all to see on his handsome, but aging, overly tanned face. He was a man in his mid-fifties who looked a whole lot older.

He was also a mess of drink and cocaine. He could carry neither substance with style nor dignity. Anytime he got drunk or stoned he was a fucking lunatic. Which was often, on both counts. But in wrestling he was a draw. He was someone the people were willing to pay to see no matter what territory he was in. In his business he had done it all—except be World Heavyweight Champion.

He nervously walked to the designated back door and was immediately recognized by a starstruck rookie wrestler who got the job of doorman. Shane tipped him with a hundred. He tipped everyone, all the time. He slowly took the steep stairs and waited to reclaim his breath when he reached the top. He fixed his hair and made sure all his jewelry was facing the right way. The sounds inside were muted but large. He knew it was a full room of scumbags doing their best not to enjoy themselves too much in front of the boss who held all the power in the wrestling business.

It was a long time since Shane Montrose had been nervous.

But this time he had good reason to be.

In the dirty restroom, Danno robotically washed his hands. Most everything he did now was on autopilot. The restroom door opened and Joe Lapine, the chairman of the NWC, entered. Danno watched in the mirror as Joe stood with the stall door open and took a piss.

"How are you holding up, Danno?" Joe asked.

Danno didn't know how to answer such a question. So he didn't.

"I don't even know what to say to you," Joe said as he finished up. "It's a tragedy." He flushed and took up a spot washing in the sink next to Danno.

Danno realized he had washed his hands twenty times over and the cuffs of his shirt were soaking wet.

"I wanted to stay with you last night," Joe said as he checked to make sure the stalls were empty. "Because no man should go through that alone."

Danno never even looked up.

Joe caught Danno's eye in the mirror.

"I appreciate you giving me the chair when you could have taken it for yourself. So I'm glad we could set that Proctor *meeting* for you," Joe said.

Danno rubbed his hands on the worn-out towel that was barely clinging to the wall.

"Someone said you . . ." Joe stopped and looked around again. "Did the deed?"

Joe could clearly see that Danno didn't want to talk about it, so he changed the subject. "Now, we all just want to help you move on, Danno."

"Move on?" Danno asked, his voice raspy from lack of use.

"Move on," Joe reiterated. "To get back to business."

Danno cleared his throat so there would be no misunderstanding in what he was about to say. "You think I'm finished looking for him, Joe?"

"We hope that you are. All of us. It's best for business."

Danno dried his hands, reached for the door, and walked back into the packed room.

Joe said, "The National Wrestling Council stands with—"

Danno was gone and Joe didn't even bother to finish his sentence.

January 10, 1969.
Three years before Annie's murder.
Oregon.

Danno sat among the National Wrestling Council—a collection of men who owned the largest wrestling territories in the Americas—and looked around at all the faces at the table. It was their job to fuck people over, keep competitors out, and make as much cash money as they possibly could from match-fixing professional wrestling contests. It was this collection of scam artists, backstabbers, and ruthless businessmen who would decide his long-term legacy. Danno wanted the champion in his territory, and in his business a champion wasn't crowned in the ring; he was anointed at the NWC table.

"We move on to the world heavyweight champion," Merv Schiller said. "Danno Garland wants the belt to come to New York where he has that giant waiting."

All the other bosses smiled and nodded in Danno's direction.

Merv lifted his glasses from his nose to read. "The National Wrestling Council has decided via traditional unanimous vote that there will be no change in the . . ."

Danno was devastated. The people around him looked to be shocked at the outcome, but he knew they were snakes and liars.

He watched Merv's mouth moving and other bosses shouting in feigned outrage, but time moved slowly and quietly for Danno. His stomach turned, his mouth ran dry. He knew he'd just been fucked over. And that meant millions of dollars had just evaporated.

Annie Garland sat in the foyer, half reading from her book and half watching the door. She looked out for any sign of Danno—although she knew it would be hours yet before he returned from his big meeting. Her heart was full with excitement. And guilt. But she felt she couldn't help it. For days she had tossed the word "compelled" around in her head. That was all she could think to call her wants. She felt, and was, compelled.

"You ready?" whispered a moving voice behind her.

Annie took one last look at the giant glass front door and satisfied herself that the coast was clear. She quickly followed Shane Montrose into the waiting elevator.

Shane hurriedly opened the door to his room and scooped Annie off her feet. His wrestling dates had kept them apart for the best part of a year. She adored him, missed him. She loved him. She wondered if he felt the same. He must have. He made it his business to get to Oregon. To her.

He'd been a mercenary his whole career. He traveled where the best money was and he never had any problems letting the bosses know that. He was a rare thing in the wrestling business in that he got over with the audience no matter how many times a promoter tried to make an example out of him by making him lose. He once lost four straight title matches in the same building and he still managed to sell it out the next week. And he did it all with a microphone. He knew how to make people feel the way he wanted them to feel. He knew how to garner sympathy and rally soldiers of support in the stands. He could do what all truly great wrestlers could—he could manipulate people. The bosses loved that. Manipulated people spent money.

Annie knew it wasn't a coincidence that he was here at the same time the NWC was meeting here. Still, she let herself be fooled, let herself believe he was there only for her.

"Okay, let's move on to any other business," Merv said as he pulled his glasses from his forehead and shuffled some papers.

Danno cleared his throat, and the meeting left a respectful silence for his potential input. He stood up.

"We had a deal, Merv." Danno looked around the room to see which of the other eight owners had knifed him in the back. "But more than that, I have someone who we know people are going to pay to see. I have someone who you all watched work a few months ago—someone who could make us all a lot of money. Now I've kept him off TV, kept his appearances low profile, because I was waiting for the nod today. I was going to explode this kid onto the scene and get the world talking."

"He was green as goose shit and we need to move on to other business, Danno," Merv interrupted.

"But I have a question," Danno fired back.

"Make it quick," Merv said.

Fuck it. Danno had nothing to gain anymore by being polite anyway. "Yeah, just one point. Would you still be reneging on our deal if the giant jumped to your company like you quietly offered him to do several times last week?"

The occupants of the room turned squarely to Merv to hear his response. Danno had simply asked what everyone else was thinking. Merv sputtered, "In my life, I've never been so insulted and . . . and . . . what's the word?"

Danno instinctively finished his sentence. "Crooked?"

Merv picked up his ashtray and unsuccessfully threw it at Danno's head. "You be fucking careful what you lay at my door, you Mick fuck. Where's your evidence that I tried to sign your guy? You didn't get the belt today 'cause you'd only fuck it up if you did. Simple as that."

Danno could have been standing in front of his old man. The same old man who kept him away from the business at every turn. The same man who trusted Danno with nothing and left him even less when he died.

You didn't get the business, Danno, 'cause you'd only fuck it up if you did.

Annie lay on the bed and watched one of the most famous wrestlers in the world tear at his clothes. His body was a little softer than she remembered. The road—and time—was taking its toll.

Shane smiled at her and tried to hide the fact that various injuries wouldn't let him get down far enough to take his socks off.

The hotel room, the running around, the planning, the danger. Back home it kept Annie going. She cherished the flutter it gave her. But here, in reality, it made her feel sick. Danno was a good man. Solid. Measured. Predictable. A little boring. But good.

"I can't," she said as she whipped herself from the bed.

"What?" Shane replied.

"I can't," she repeated as she dropped her head in shame and made her way to the door. "I'm sorry."

"Wait, baby. What's going on here?"

"I'm sorry. I don't know what I'm doing."

She managed to break away from this once before. Things were getting better at home. She didn't know what made her say yes to see him again.

History and chemistry were a dangerous combination.

"Well?" Merv glared at Danno, "Are we moving this meeting on?"

Danno hesitantly nodded. There would be no celebration, no victory speech, and no blowjob from Missus Garland that night.

Merv, in turn, also sat down. "I was going to inform the meeting that Sal was going to tour your territories again this summer as champion. Boost your gates."

The other owners smiled and nodded at the scrap of generosity, and everyone turned attentively to his next item. Everyone except Proctor King, who winked at Danno.

Business was about to pick up.

All the real meetings took place after the meeting. All the owners knew this but never said anything. The planning, scheming, the hush-hush handshakes, all took place an hour after everyone left to "go home." This was when Merv Schiller, as chairman of the NWC, normally held court, cut deals, and generally protected his spot.

Merv wasn't the only one who was at a meeting.

Danno's took place with an unlikely ally in Proctor King. They had never had much, if any, dealing with each other in the past. Proctor's request for a meeting was unusual, to say the least. He took it because he just didn't want to go back home a failure again. He didn't want to have that talk with his wife again. He couldn't. He was too old to be an also-ran.

So he waited in the restaurant.

The one man without a meeting was Curt Magee.

Same old shit, same old fucking shit, he thought as he lowered another beer and wiped the foam from his white mustache.

He skimmed and re-skimmed the meeting from earlier in his mind. The way he had been spoken to. The disrespect of cutting a grown man out of his livelihood. He knew that they were all planning a meeting without him. Curt's territory was hurting more than most. He needed a slice of the money that old Merv was funneling off for himself. But he knew he wasn't in Merv's troop—or any other troop. That left Curt very vulnerable.

To keep your place at the NWC table you had to be valuable. Curt was just about out of any worth—within the NWC or his own goddamn house.

He squinted at the figure at the end of the bar. "Shane?" he muttered.

At the other end of the Governor Hotel bar, the Sugarstick, Shane Montrose, was lowering shot after shot. Curt didn't recognize him at first. Partly because his sight was bad, and partly because he'd never been in a bar with Shane Montrose where the Sugarstick was so quiet and somber.

"Well, fuck me," Curt said as he walked closer.

Shane barely looked up from his glass. "Curt Magee, the famous owner from Texas in these United States of America."

Curt dragged up a stool. "What are you doing here?"

"Fishing. What do you think I'm doing in a fucking bar? I'm knitting a hat."

"Okay, I was only asking," Curt said.

Shane downed another shot and slammed his glass off the bar. "How many wrestlers did you all fuck over today?" Shane asked.

"What?"

"At your big meeting. How many of us did you guys fuck over? Did you cut our payoffs some more, or trade us like the fucking cattle you think we are?" Shane slipped uneasily off his stool and clawed at his shirt, ripping all the buttons off. He struggled to pull his tailor-made jacket over his head, but only succeeded in trapping himself. "Fucking help me," Shane said in a panicked, high-pitched voice.

Curt grabbed the jacket and Shane burrowed himself backwards out of it. Curt became more aware of the scene they were creating. "What are you doing?"

"Freeing myself," Shane replied as he unhooked his belt.

Curt grabbed his arm. "People are watching."

"Fucking good." Shane pulled away from Curt and fell into an empty table behind him.

Proctor didn't feel at ease in the restaurant, so he made Danno come outside the Old Spaghetti Factory and slide down the bank by the river. Now it was Danno who was ill at ease. There was no one around. That was what Proctor wanted. Danno, not so much.

"Nice view, huh?"

Danno tried to assess the situation and the geography without making it obvious he was doing so. He also watched the water's edge so as not to get his feet wet. "What did you want to see me about?" Danno asked.

"I want to do some business that will make us both rich." Proctor inhaled before continuing. "Big money."

"Haven't you got an office or a phone for this kind of stuff?" Danno asked.

"Not this kinda stuff."

Proctor waited for Danno's response and enjoyed the power of watching Danno digest the broken information.

"Well?" Danno asked. "What are we talking about here?"

Proctor took one last look up the bank before gravitating toward Danno's ear. "I want to get you the belt."

Danno leaned back to recapture his personal space. "You were there today, Proctor. You saw the room vote with Merv. Maybe you voted with him too. I don't fucking know who is with who in that room."

Proctor smiled and nodded at Danno's naïveté. "Fuck Merv and those monkeys who follow him. I can get you the belt by the end of the month. That'll give you time to put a program in place for that giant golden goose you found—you lucky bastard."

Curt and Shane sat in a booth in the bar. Shane was wearing just his jacket, underwear, black knee socks, and shiny dress shoes. This arrangement seemed to have calmed him.

"Merv got me," Shane said as he suckled a beer bottle. "He said I was the greatest of all time. The best wrestler to never have the heavyweight title. I agree with him there."

Curt also nodded in agreement. Everyone knew it.

Montrose continued, "Merv said he was putting together the biggest match of them all. He got me to leave Tanner and come with him to San Francisco. I moved the family. Laid down some money on a nice house, put my kid in a new school. It was finally going to happen for me. He promised me the belt. Now he's fucking avoiding me. He won't even book me on his cards."

It took Curt all of two seconds to figure out why Merv would keep one of the best of all time on the shelf. What Shane was saying clicked with what Curt had heard at the NWC meeting earlier.

Merv had tried to sign Babu the giant from under Danno's nose. He was wanting to put together the most popular wrestler never to be champion, Shane Montrose, versus the new giant. Montrose trained the giant, broke him into the wrestling business. Teacher versus student. Experience versus youth. The rightful champion versus the new unstoppable giant. It was perfect. It was also a gold mine.

"Does he have a contract with you?" Curt asked.

Shane nodded. "Long term. You know how these things work, Curt. I'm fucked."

"Jesus."

"Things are not good. I owe the IRS, two ex-wives, and a couple of failing businesses. I'm selling my things to get by. Boots, trunks, anything they'll buy."

Curt saw the opening he was looking for.

"Merv is a greedy pig. He wants to collect all the talent and put them on the shelf so no one else can have them."

"Yeah, well, the way you guys have this game stacked—we only get paid when we work. And I can't live on fresh air and hollow promises."

Curt and Shane sat side by side, both feeling cheated, both making little money, and both thinking what a greedy little prick Merv was.

Curt made absolutely sure that no one from inside the wrestling business was around before he leaned over to Shane's ear. "Why don't you come work for me?"

Shane looked at Curt skeptically. He'd heard that one before.

"Fuck Merv," Curt whispered.

Owners didn't talk like that about other owners. Particularly in front of wrestlers. Shane was drunk, but not drunk enough to not be worried that someone might hear.

"He's got my contract," Shane said.

"What if I could do something that made us rich?" Curt knew that Merv was trying to have all the cake. Merv wanted to own Shane Montrose and the giant. Curt didn't consider himself that greedy. If Danno Garland had the giant, then Curt could snap up the challenger and they'd have to work together. Half the box office of the biggest match of all time was better than none of the box office of the biggest match of all time.

Curt wasn't comfortable in the open. He signaled for the Sugarstick to follow him into the small hallway off the restrooms.

"I'll sign you. We'll make the match. You versus the giant. We get half and Danno gets half. We do the match all over the country. There's more money there than any other match."

"What about Merv?" Montrose asked.

Curt took a swig of his drink. His hands were shaking. They did that a lot when he got excited or angry. "I'll straighten Merv out. I'd be doing everyone a favor."

"It's a win-win." Proctor flicked his exhausted cigarette butt into the river. "We got a deal?"

Danno felt he needed more time. It made total sense as Proctor laid it out, but he knew this was as close as his mortal self was ever going to get to shaking hands with the devil.

"Danno?" The pitch of Proctor's voice raised—he was seemingly surprised that he had to chase an answer.

Danno opened his mouth and paused. Even if it meant getting himself in even further with Proctor, money and fancy underbritches were powerful motivation.

"On one condition," Danno said, the water now running over his feet.

"What's that?"

"I call the angle when the time comes."

Proctor smiled and offered a handshake.

Proctor and Danno shook hands.

"Deal?" Curt asked.

Shane warily thought about what they were getting into. Merv left him no choice.

"On one condition," Shane said.

"What's that?" Curt asked.

"I work *with* you. Not *for* you. We become partners."

Curt saw five more years of work left in Shane's faltering body. If he could pull off a deal with Danno, they would be the five most lucrative years of all their lives. If he couldn't . . . Curt didn't even want to entertain that thought. There was only one match out there that made any sense. And Curt Magee was about to outthink them all for once and own half of it.

"Deal," Curt said.

Shane put out his hand, "Don't you ever try and fuck me over, lie to me, or cheat me out of a payoff."

"I won't."

Shane leaned in. "'Cause I'll fucking kill you if you do."

Both men had an understanding.

Curt finished his drink. "Anything I should know before we do this?"

"Like what?" Shane asked.

"Just anything you think I should know."

Shane shook his head. He knew there was something Curt should know.

"Okay. Deal," Curt said.

Curt and the Sugarstick, Shane Montrose, shook hands. Professional wrestling was littered with bad handshakes, but this particular one ranked at the very top.

"Can you settle my bar tab?" Shane asked. "I have no money."

October 10, 1972.
Four days after Annie's murder.
New York.

Shane slowly walked the back room toward Danno with his head bowed. He didn't know who knew what—if anything at all. He'd hoped that the fact he was still walking around meant Danno didn't know. He was petrified, but not coming would only make things worse. So there he was, like a shameful dog, walking across the floor at Annie Garland's wake.

"Sit down," Danno said without raising his head from thought.

Shane did just that. "I'm sorry about . . ."

"Do you know where Curt Magee is?" Danno asked directly.

"No, I swear to God. I swear on my kid's life."

Danno opened his hand and showed him a tangled ball of rosary beads. "This is what they gave me. They took her and put her in the ground and this is the receipt."

"I'm sorry," Shane said, trying to hold back his tears. "I'm sorry."

Danno broke his stare from the floor and lifted his head. All the other mourners were sliding past the "respect" phase of the wake and moving into the louder, more drunken part.

"They get you when you're a kid," Danno started. "And they put all this stuff in your head about devils and fire and clouds and light. And I can't fucking shake it. I can't carve the bullshit they put in there out of my head."

"Danno . . ."

Danno slammed his fist on the table. The whole room stopped dead. "What are you looking at?" Danno asked the gossipy room. He leaned into Shane Montrose. "I knew and I . . . accepted."

"Accepted what?" Shane asked.

"None of your fucking lies," Danno said as he dropped the rosary beads.

Shane drew a large breath and clasped his hands on the table. He leaned in closer. "I loved her."

Those words, this day, no sleep, no joy. Danno did nothing.

Shane continued. "I loved her and I respected her. And my heart is broke over what happened. I want to help you find Curt."

Danno watched Shane's eyes fill up with tears. He then slid his gaze around the filthy, smoky room. Danno Garland and Shane Montrose were the only two in the room who really felt something for Annie.

Shane began to well up. "I'm ashamed of what I did. I'm ashamed and it makes me sick to my stomach. It wasn't . . . it just got out of hand. I'm sorry, Danno." Shane grabbed Danno's hand and dropped from his seat to his knee. "I'm sorry."

The room tried to pretend it wasn't looking at the scene unfolding at the top of the room. Danno wanted to kill him—he wanted to stand up and thrust his fingers into his eyes and overturn the heavy table on the side of his head. He wanted to stomp Shane and stab at him and choke him and bite his face. "Get up."

Shane looked up from his bended knee. "I'm sorry."

"Get up, I said."

Shane warily rose to his feet.

Danno stood and shouted for the room to listen. "Curt didn't fucking do this on his own," Danno shouted as he turned one by one around his fellow bosses. "I want you all to hear me when I say this." The room was deathly quiet. Danno couldn't have picked a more awkward and uncomfortable day or place to unload. "My only business left is to make sure whoever did this to . . ." He couldn't bring himself to say his wife's name. ". . . to make sure whoever . . . every-fucking-person who was involved in this dies. Then I'll lie down and you vultures can pick away whatever's left." Danno looked at all the hung heads in front of him. "For years you all wanted me to get my hands dirty. Well, fuck you—they're dirty now." Danno downed his shot, threw his glass against the wall, and walked toward the door. "I'll give a hundred thousand dollars to anyone who leads me to Curt Magee," he said before he left.

Joe Lapine shook his head in disbelief. There was only so big of a crack he could smooth over as Chair of the NWC. An outburst like this, in public, and in front of the wrestlers, was sure to incense the other bosses.

"Did he just place a bounty? In here?" Tanner Blackwell, the Carolina boss, mouthed to Joe in anger.

Joe nodded in disbelief.

Shane Montrose reached into his pocket. He took out a ball of hundreds and walked to the bar. "This is on me. All of it."

He wanted to see if it was possible to spend his guilt away. He had a lot of money and a lot of guilt.

CHAPTER FIVE

Ginny lay somewhere. He wasn't sure where, but he knew he was dressed in a suit. He waited. Waiting always helped the fog to clear from his head. He was totally confused, but at least he still had the advantage of understanding what was happening to him. It was an episode; something that would pass. He hoped. He found it hard to verbalize. A proud, old-school man like Ginny didn't feel like talking about himself at the best of times.

This was not the best of times.

He waited for some familiarity to come back to him. Something to latch onto and make his anxiety pass. Make his surroundings known to him. The voice shouting at him from the other side of the door wasn't making things any better.

"Sir?"

That voice wouldn't go away. It was, in fact, getting more impatient.

"NYPD. Open the door," demanded the voice outside.

Ginny didn't move, and he didn't open the door. For six hours he lay on the floor of his apartment. He remembered and forgot again just why he was there. For a man as tough and as strong as he used to be, Ginny had never felt quite as scared in his whole life. He was lying, curled into a ball, with no memory of how he got there; an overbearing feeling of horror and not knowing what he was afraid of; anger at finding himself afraid again; and shame at not being able to do anything about it.

He lay there, just wishing for Ricky to come home. He lay there not knowing if anyone loved him. He lay there like a child lies quietly in their bed. All he knew to do was just lie there. A scared stranger—in his own apartment.

Ricky Plick walked along West Forty-Second and stopped at a familiar midsized building. The sun was high in the sky over Manhattan and Ricky knew he still had a long day ahead of him. With Danno so focused on other matters, it was up to Ricky to erase all the incriminating breadcrumbs leading back their way. Especially after Danno's announcement at Annie's wake. If the bosses weren't out to get Danno before, they sure as fuck were now. No single boss could put out a bounty on the whereabouts of another boss without it raising serious eyebrows, regardless of what happened.

Ricky entered the building and pulled his collar up nice and high over his face. He took the elevator to the third floor and walked down a corridor lined with offices. He stopped at a door he rarely entered.

THE NEW YORK BOOKING AGENCY.

Danno's office.

Ricky inserted the key he had taken from Danno and moved it very slowly and quietly in the lock. *Click.*

He looked behind him before entering.

After what Danno had done to Proctor, and how recklessly he had done it, Ricky needed to make sure that he disappeared anything that could incriminate them, anything that could lead anyone back to Danno. That was his job. That was who he was as a person. Ricky was loyal and was looking after his boss's best interests even when his boss wasn't.

He opened the office door and navigated the room. He would have preferred to do this type of thing under cover of darkness, but he didn't have that luxury. Even though Ricky had visited this office before, he had never done so with an empty bag on his back and a stolen key in his pocket. He was certainly Danno's number two— but he stayed far away from "the paperwork."

This office was the place that made Danno officially who he was. To exist in New York and stay under the radar, Danno had to run a "real" company. He had to have the papers to say that he owned what he owned. He had contracts with TV companies, wrestlers, and the venues. He had to prove he paid taxes. That he had employees. His company was listed at this address, under his name.

That was the official bit. The front.

Behind that was the *actual* business. The cash money, under-the-table business that he ran with the other bosses. The *actual* business fixed matches and bribed anyone who could make that pursuit easier. Cash passed under the table to wrestlers as well as fellow bosses, local TV owners, the guys that ran the buildings, some newspaper guys, a fire chief or two, and a couple of cops from Danno's father's day.

That was a lot of money moving back and forth. Everyone in the wrestling business was connected through a web of paper, IOUs, contracts, and deals.

The phone rang and an answering machine kicked in right away. "Hello, you have reached the New York Booking Agency, the home of the world's greatest wrestling attractions. We are unable to come to the phone right now so please leave a message and we will get back to you as soon as possible. Thank you."

Beep.

The caller hung up.

Another thing Ricky had learned through the years was how to pay close attention without anyone noticing. The details, the subtleties. Ricky had a head full of things that most everyone else forgot.

Danno's office was at the end of the room. Ricky pushed the door open, entered, and quickly knelt down at the side of the huge desk.

He took a paranoid look around before pulling back the thin rug. He then popped his finger down an inconspicuous hole in the floorboard and gently pulled. A perfect square lifted and exposed a safe recessed into the floor. Ricky turned the numbered dial in a few different directions and opened the thick metal door.

Ricky's bag was already open and waiting. He removed five thousand dollars and placed it in the bag. Even with the money removed, Ricky saw that there was plenty more waiting in there. He figured maybe seventy or eighty thousand. He quietly rearranged everything to hide he'd been there, closed the safe, and fixed the thin rug back in place. Ricky stood and walked lightly out of Danno's dark office with a short stack of Danno's money for insurance.

If Ricky couldn't talk Danno off the road he was on, he was at least going to try to cover the tracks he was leaving behind.

Nevada.

Lenny guided Luke and James Henry across the parking lot of their motel. Luke had the ability to wander but James Henry still needed carrying over distances. Lenny also had a third item that needed careful attention: his wrestling magazine.

Although making his way in the wrestling business almost broke up his family and destroyed his marriage, Lenny couldn't help but pine for it. He knew his spot in that closed-off world was a one-in-a-million chance, and he couldn't shake the feeling that he was missing out, that the circus was leaving town without him. Or, more pointedly, that he skipped out on the circus and now couldn't find a way back in.

Ever since he got involved, Lenny had been looking for a way to come home. For it to not be weird. For his wife to love him. For his kids to know him. But wrestling overtook all of that. It consumed him.

No one saw that more than his wife. Bree Long, the only woman in history who ran away from her marriage, and collected her husband along the way.

Lenny packed up the job he loved to come out West with his family. He just drew the line at staying with Bree's parents. He wanted to be his own, make an effort to pull his family back together first. Get his wife her rings back. Do things right.

So it was motel living for the Longs until Lenny figured everything out.

"Hello?" Lenny said as he slowly entered their room.

Bree was sobbing on the bed in her casino uniform.

"What's wrong?" Lenny asked as he quickly knelt down in front of her. "Honey?" Lenny asked again, trying to get her to lift her head from her hands.

"It's Dad," Bree replied through her tears.

Lenny picked up on the fact that she was reluctant to continue with the children right there listening.

"Kids, go and wait in the car," Lenny said as he passed the two-year-old into the arms of the seven-year-old.

Bree interrupted. "You can't send them outside, Lenny. Jesus." She wiped her face, got up and turned on the TV, cracked open the candy stash, and had them both distracted and quiet in seconds.

Lenny tried to rub her back as she moved, but only ended up in her way. "What's the matter with your father?" Lenny whispered.

"Mom said he's had a stroke. I called them on my break and she was just home from the hospital to get some of his things."

"Jesus, that's terrible," Lenny said as he tried to embrace her. Bree was already throwing her clothes into a bag.

"I've got to go," she said.

"Where?"

"To my folks, Lenny."

"Yeah, of course."

Bree stopped and looked at her husband. "I've got a friend who said she would watch the kids."

"They can't go with you?" Lenny asked.

"I can't bring the kids to see their grandfather like that."

Lenny whispered, "Has he got the face thing?"

Bree nodded. Her heart was broken.

"You should go," Lenny said. "You should do the right thing here. I could . . . I could watch the kids."

Bree wasn't sure at all.

Lenny gently took her by her shoulders and looked her in the eyes. "I can follow you with the kids in a week or so. It'll give you time, and your dad time, and your mom time, to focus on getting better."

Bree nodded. She just wanted to go. If she left now she could be there before the morning. "You sure?"

Lenny nodded. "Of course. I meant it when I said I want to be better for this family."

Bree dried her eyes and hugged her husband tightly. She knew their kids barely knew him but maybe this time together alone would help that.

"Do you know where my folks live?" she asked.

"I'll find you," Lenny said. "I'll knock every door on the street if I have to. And I'll bring a surprise."

"What surprise?" she asked.

"You'll see."

"I'm kinda afraid that you're going to leave our kids on a bus or something."

Lenny kissed his wife. "I promise not to leave them on a bus." He took her hand and kissed her bare ring finger. "I'm sorry—"

"It doesn't matter," Bree said, interrupting him. She stood and drew breath as she began to formulate her thoughts.

"Anything else I can do?" Lenny asked.

She smiled and shook her head. Lenny could see her eye was drawn to where he had found the money earlier. He made sure to stand right in front of the cabinet so Bree wouldn't have a chance to see it was now gone. He had a plan for that money. A plan to fix the one thing he regretted most. A plan to close the door on his old life.

A plan to help his wife to love him again.

January 21, 1969.
Three years before Annie's murder.
Memphis.

Today was the fucking day. Curt Magee, the boss of the Texas territory, was finally going to get him some. He had worked out a provisional fifty-fifty split with one of wrestling's biggest stars—the Sugarstick, Shane Montrose—to come join his company. Curt even agreed to pay a hundred and fifty grand up front for the services of the Sugarstick, as he was the top draw in his territory. Mrs. Magee didn't agree with her ex-husband putting their old house on the line to sign a wrestler, but fuck her, it wasn't like they were together anymore anyways.

For once in his life, Curt felt smarter than all the other bosses. Danno might have the champion but Curt was putting together a plan to swipe the obvious next challenger for himself. Champions weren't worth shit without an opponent—someone the public would pay to see them wrestle. Curt figured that would be Shane Montrose. All Curt had to do was remove his biggest obstacle, the National Wrestling Council chairman, Merv Schiller, and the Sugarstick was all his. So he waited at the end of Thomas Street to do just that.

Curt wasn't quite sure how the plan was going to go. All he knew was he was to meet a man his cousin had lined up. Curt had a sense that Thomas Street was a bad part of town to meet a stranger to exchange a handful of money.

Most of the other bosses were former wrestlers or college football stars who could look after themselves. Curt, like Danno Garland, had no such pedigree. That's why he had brought along a handgun for company, just in case this all went to shit. He watched his side mirrors studiously for anyone approaching from behind. His anxiety was only heightened by that silence you only get from an empty street. His bladder felt fuller as the minutes ticked by. He'd gone to piss twice but the nervous wait made him feel like he needed to piss again. The eventual sound of metal tapping on glass nearly made him empty himself completely. So much for his active mirror watching.

"Are you the guy?" a voice asked from the outside.

Curt composed himself and rolled down the passenger window a little. "Are *you* the guy?"

"I am, if you're the guy."

"Yeah, I'm the guy," Curt answered with his hand over his face.

"Gimme the money."

"Up front?"

The man outside laughed. "You think I'm going to do this and then jog back here so you can pay me?"

Curt watched Merv step out from the American Sound Studio. He took a bag of cash from his glove box and pushed it through the small crack in the window. "The old guy. Up there."

"Him outside the studio?"

"Yeah."

Curt and the hooded man outside his car looked up the street at the little old guy hanging off the end of his huge cigar. He looked frail and harmless and no trouble to anyone.

"You don't know him. He's a fucking . . . asshole," Curt said, feeling the need to justify his decision.

The man outside the car began to laugh. "Man, I don't give a shit. You say he's the guy, then he's the guy."

Curt's new acquaintance walked away from the car and reached inside his coat as he approached an unsuspecting Merv. He grasped the cold metal as Merv flicked the cigar butt into the street and turned toward his approaching driver. The hired guy sped up his stride and took to the sidewalk where Merv had clasped his hands under his armpits and danced on the spot.

As the lights of his approaching car shone on him, Merv's head was cracked open from behind by a tire iron.

"Holy fuck," Curt muttered to himself as he saw it unfold. He knew what was going to happen but was still shocked to see it actually play out.

Merv's chauffeured car stuttered to a stop and his driver got out and ran toward his boss, who was lifeless on the ground. Merv's fresh, plentiful blood surged along the curb and pooled beside his gloved hand.

In the darkness a few hundred feet away, Curt calmly rolled his car back without any lights on. He didn't think of prison or of Merv's family. As he drove off the opposite way on Thomas Street in Memphis, Tennessee, Curt Magee thought about money.

October 10, 1972.
Four days after Annie's murder.
New York.

Ricky covertly took Danno's used .38 Special from his pocket. Ginny had told him that cops had come knocking but that he couldn't remember why. And he didn't know when. It sounded close. Too close. So Ricky threw Danno's used gun into the dark waters of the East River in front of him.

Gone was one piece of evidence from the night Ricky never wanted to remember again. He only had one more piece left to get rid of. The five grand he had in his car was to make sure that large piece of evidence was taken care of too.

He rested his forearms on the railing and filled his lungs with air and his eyes with the city. He liked it best at a distance, so he could appreciate the sight without the noise. Each window made him think of someone working or a deal being done. Money changing hands. People running for the elevator with their briefcases hanging by the straps from their mouths and papers falling out from under their arms. The buildings, the lapping water, and the muted mayhem across the river. Brooklyn Promenade gave him a sense of perspective on Manhattan and other, more personal things.

"How much higher can they build those fucking things?" Joe Lapine asked as he stood beside Ricky and looked at the city across the water.

Both men focused on the two new identical structures that now dominated the cityscape.

"They're done. The tallest in the world," Ricky said and bit into his homemade sandwich. "A hundred and ten stories."

"Who the fuck needs a hundred and ten stories?" Joe asked like the visitor he was.

Ricky watched Joe survey the area. "He's not here," Ricky said of Danno. "And we're taping our TV shows in a couple of hours, so I have to get out of here soon."

No one else was there. The men had the place to themselves, to speak openly.

"How is he doing?" Joe asked, about Danno.

"He's good," Ricky said, lying through his teeth. He walked back from the railing and sat on one of the wooden benches near the bushes. Joe sauntered across too.

"How's business?" Joe asked.

On that one, Ricky couldn't lie. "Not great."

Danno had appointed Joe Lapine acting chair of the National Wrestling Council when Merv got murdered. Danno wanted the champion, the money, and extra territories. But taking the chair right after Merv was killed would have raised some eyebrows about if he was the man who ordered the kill. So Danno asked Joe, the seemingly levelheaded boss in Memphis, to keep the seat warm until things calmed down.

But things never calmed down.

It was an arrangement that suited both men. Joe ran the meetings and took over the collective business while Danno had the power and money of being the boss with the champion.

"There are concerns for everyone involved. The other bosses are still over there," Joe said, nodding to the city. "And nobody is happy. Especially after the shit Danno pulled today."

"What shit?" Ricky asked.

"You didn't hear? He put a fucking bounty on Curt Magee. In front of everyone."

Ricky was stunned—not that he'd ever let Joe see that. "He's the man, Joe. He's got the belt and he's got the territories. The rest of you are going to have to give him time to get back on his feet." Ricky stood up. "Do you mind walking?"

Ginny was waiting for Ricky in their car and Ricky didn't want to leave him too long. The men began to stroll.

Joe said, "The bosses have called a meeting at midnight tonight. They want to hear your plans. We even have the foreign bosses asking what's going on. In a chain like ours, one of us could pull the rest down with him. You know this as well as anyone."

"I understand," Ricky replied.

"There's a trust issue forming," Joe said.

Ricky stopped and laughed at the suggestion. These bosses never trusted each other, not a single inch for a single second. They all knew the business. They sat in a tight circle and every one of them had a bare neck and a sharp blade. It was only a matter of who sliced who first.

"Danno's got it under control," Ricky dutifully lied.

"Does Danno sound like someone who has it under control, Ricky?" Joe blew into his hands and slapped them together. "I'm not like Merv. You should probably know that. I take being chairman of the National Wrestling Council very serious. Now, I know Danno has got the most turf and he has the champion. But my job is to make this thing we have fair and equitable for all involved. Your business is a mess right now. And Danno's thing is at the heart of that."

"His *thing*?"

"His personal matters. It's all drawing a lot of attention our way. On all of our houses. He's making accusations and threats against the other bosses. He should have never done the deal under the table with Proctor. The riot in Shea, the senator getting knifed . . . Danno's wife. It's all coming from *your* territory."

How could Ricky argue? "We'll fix it."

Joe was adamant that Ricky hear everything he had to say. "We can't do our jobs if people employed by the government are looking too closely at us. Senators, the Athletic Commission, cops. We need New York to go quiet. I'm saying not a fucking peep. Let this all pass without any more incidents."

"Is that what you'd do?" Ricky asked. "Your wife comes up dead in a hotel somewhere and you'd just drop it for the good of the business?"

"He got his peace. We all made sure of that," Joe said, reminding Ricky of Proctor's demise only the night before. "He has used up all his rope on this matter. You'd be wise to let him know that."

Ricky listened carefully. He couldn't argue with anything that Joe, as chairman of the NWC, was saying. He just had a feeling that Joe mightn't have anyone else's best interests at heart, either.

"He's got this, Joe," Ricky said.

Joe buttoned his long overcoat up to his neck. "How much longer do you think the other bosses are going to allow this to go on? Danno making threats? Putting money out for people inside this business to be killed?" he asked. "For a hundred years we've tip-toed around, made our money, and kept to ourselves. We're fucking promoters. We're not in the killing business. If someone has an issue with someone then they need to sort it out outside of our deal. If someone needs to be taught some manners or something, we do it amongst ourselves and we do it for the good of the business. Danno wants to put a powder keg in the middle of our livelihoods and he doesn't care what the outcome is. If he doesn't pull back it's going to arrive at all of our doors. Don't *make* me do something about this, Ricky."

Joe walked away.

Nestor watched Ricky and Joe from a neighboring bench. He wondered if Ricky Plick would remember his face if they locked eyes. The time wasn't right to find out just yet, so Nestor turned away as Ricky walked past him.

April 16, 1969.
Three years before Annie's murder.
New York.

All the windows in the house were shattered and the smell of burned leather and melted rubber was still everywhere. Nosy neighbors kept finding reasons to walk past the house at regular intervals.

But Danno had given Ricky his orders. Make sure the investigation didn't go anywhere.

"That's a real shame," the detective said as he and Ricky stood in the driveway beside the smoldering Cadillac. "Coupe DeVille?"

"Was," Ricky said.

"Anyone in the house see anything? See anyone hanging around?"

"No," Ricky answered.

"'Cause we got some eyewitnesses down the street here, saying they saw a dark-colored car heading out of here quick. We think we got an eyewitness account of the driver."

Ricky knew he needed to counter quickly. Danno was in league with Proctor King on the biggest deal in wrestling history, and the last thing anyone wanted was Proctor or his guys arrested. As Danno told Ricky earlier, "This is an internal matter that will be dealt with our own way."

"It was my fault," Ricky said.

"You did this?" the detective asked as he looked at the charred car beside them.

"I got in earlier with a smoke and the tip must've fallen off. The interior on these cars is way too flammable."

The detective laughed a little as he took his notes. "So you burned your boss's car down with a wayward smoke?"

"Unfortunately so."

"He must be pissed about that. Can I talk to him?"

Ricky smiled. "He's inside comforting his wife. She got quite the fright, I'm not proud to say."

Both men paused for a second.

"Can I ask your boss's name?" the detective asked.

"Danno. Garland."

The detective wrote it down.

"And yours?" Ricky asked.

"Detective Chapman. Nestor," the detective said as he handed over his card.

"Well, Nestor. It's been a long night. Danno and his wife are more than willing to help you out with your investigation later, if that's okay."

Nestor looked over Ricky's shoulder and saw Danno monitoring everything from the hallway. "That works for me. Give my card to Mr. Garland."

"I will," Ricky said. "But there's really nothing to this. Nothing at all to concern your busy police force."

Nestor hadn't really thought so either. Until now. Something felt off. "Maybe I could have a quick word. I can see him looking out from . . ."

Ricky stood between Nestor and Danno. A move that changed Nestor's tenor completely.

"You might want to move," Nestor said.

Ricky looked around and saw there were still plenty of prying eyes. "Can I . . ." Ricky motioned for the detective to follow him to the side of the house.

Nestor followed.

"I'm in real trouble with Danno for this already," Ricky said. "He's threatening to fire me. I would be very, very grateful to you if you could just give him some space."

Ricky looked around before slowly reaching inside his coat. "I'm waiting on the window guys to get here. They asked me to leave the money outside," Ricky said as he took a generous roll of cash from his pocket. "So I'm going to leave it here."

"And you brought me around here for what?"

Ricky wasn't enjoying trying to bribe a police officer, but Danno needed this to go away. "Well, I want an officer of the law to see me leave it here, just in case it goes missing or something."

Ricky left the money on Danno's windowsill and walked away.

Nestor stared at it.

CHAPTER SIX

March 27, 1970.
Two years before Annie's murder.
New York.

Curt couldn't believe the difference. The driveway, the grounds, the house, the jealousy. He was convinced that all he had to do was wait his turn, negotiate himself a better deal, and he too could have a house like Danno. That's why he was there. That's why he turned up to Danno's new place a day before all the other bosses. He'd blame the mix-up on his secretary and get the new kingpin's ear first.

In the driveway was a simple black sedan. Danno never did get another personal car after his brand-new Cadillac got torched. He just hired himself some greenhorn named Lenny Long to take him places instead.

Curt parked his car nice and neat. "You sure you want to wait here?" he asked Shane Montrose, who was slouched in the backseat.

"Yeah, I don't even feel all that comfortable being here in the first place," Shane replied.

"You're my difference maker. He sees you and we have . . ."

"I'll follow you in," Shane said.

Curt didn't understand the sudden nervousness.

Shane said, "Gimme two secs. I'll be in. You go ahead."

Curt reluctantly got out of his car and walked to the open door. A young, skinny figure walked out to nervously meet him.

"Is Mr. Garland in?" Curt asked the rookie driver.

Lenny looked back over his shoulder and waited for direction from the hallway.

"Yes, sir. He is. Come on in," Lenny said as he stepped aside.

Curt tentatively walked into the house and took in the vastness of it, the stained wooden floors, and the sweeping staircase.

Lenny, in turn, exited and drove off in the sedan.

"Come in, Curt," Danno called from the room to Curt's right.

Curt followed the voice and peered around the door. Danno was standing, looking out the window, hands clasped behind his back, puffing on a cigar. The room was otherwise empty, with high ceilings and classic moldings on the walls. Every word bounced around and echoed on its way back out the door.

"Well, fuck me, Danno. You've got some place here," Curt said.

Danno couldn't contain his huge smile as he nodded in agreement with the Texas boss's sentiment.

"Where is everyone else?" Curt asked, already knowing the answer.

"We're all scheduled to meet tomorrow, Curt."

"Tomorrow? You sure?"

Danno moved away from the window. "Positive."

Curt offered Danno a gift. "For Mrs. Garland. I hope she likes crystal."

Danno took the present and thanked his visitor for his kindness.

Curt rubbed his tanned brown brow in fake confusion. "Shit, I was told to be here today. I'll have to fire her. I hired this honey from college. She's nice to look at but she has a memory like a goldfish."

"Let's take a look around," Danno said as he left the room.

Curt followed. "Old Mrs. Bollard used to have the memory of an elephant. Unfortunately she had the ass to match."

Curt laughed. Danno didn't.

Danno and Curt walked the grounds behind Danno's new mansion. Curt finished taking down Danno's new number into his personal pocket book. "You can't ride a horse," Curt said.

"Why not?" Danno asked.

Curt looked at Danno's growing gut and tried desperately to walk back his comment. "'Cause you can't put yourself in danger now that you've got the champion."

Danno admired Curt's attempt at a complimentary cover-up.

"I'm serious," Curt continued. "You've got the golden goose now, Danno."

Danno stopped. "What can I do for you, Curt?"

Curt had spent the last few minutes listening about bushes and trees and stables and fish ponds, all the while trying to take Danno's temperature. Was he in a good mood? Was now the right time?

"Curt?" Danno prodded.

Fuck it. No time like the present.

"I admire the way you came from the Council and took what you felt you deserved," Curt began. "I want to do the same."

Danno dropped the moist end of his cigar on the pristine lawn and stomped it into the soil. "Thanks for the compliment. But that sounds like you're planning to overthrow me."

"No, I want to follow your lead, Danno," he said. "I want to do business *with* you. Big business."

Danno picked bits of renegade tobacco from the tip of his tongue. "Let's hear it."

"I got the Sugarstick," Curt said as he whipped the contract from his inside pocket. He could hardly hold his excitement as he galloped headlong into the speech he had rehearsed a hundred times.

"We take your monster and put him in a match with his mentor—the man who brought him into this business—the Sugarstick, Shane Montrose. Your guy is the unbeatable savage that no one can stop. My guy is the white-meat babyface that has never gotten the belt. Student against teacher. My guy is the last great gunslinger mounting one more run at the belt and your guy is the unstoppable destroyer. Fuck me, can you see it? Can you smell that money? We pick the biggest venues we can get our hands on. Go around the country. Make ourselves rich. Or, you make yourself richer."

Curt waited for Danno to chime in. He didn't.

"What do you think?"

Danno didn't need to think. "Probably not."

"What?" Curt cautiously asked.

"I can't sign my guy up for that," Danno said with a new confidence in his business dealings.

The visiting Texan stumbled over his words. "Why . . . but . . ."

Danno continued. "I've got the giant signed up for something in the long run."

Curt was totally confused. "You're not sending your champion down to Texas?"

Danno knew that he couldn't politically cut Curt out. Danno was too new to make such a big play. Yet.

"No, I can send the champ down to you if you like."

A small smile started to push its way back onto Curt's face.

"But it's not for a program," Danno said. "I can send Babu down there, but he goes over strong. Your guy shows his ass—and in a squash, too."

Curt heard loud and clear. Danno wasn't going to allow any series of hard-fought matches. He was willing to let Shane Montrose and the new giant champion lock up, but Danno wanted Babu to win easily and "squash" Shane Montrose before the champion moved onto the next town.

Curt and Danno both knew that this would make Curt's new golden goose, Shane Montrose, look like a pussy.

It would give Curt a once-off payday—but would kill his territory.

In wrestling there are two ways to lose. You can lose valiantly by the skin of your teeth and have people salivating for the rematch— or you can get destroyed by an unstoppable monster and be yesterday's news. If Curt's top star had to "show ass" for the champ who was passing through his territory, then Curt would have a real tough time selling tickets with Shane's name for the remaining years on his contract. Sometimes getting the champion to town wasn't the best thing for a territory. Especially when the champion was being promoted as a "kill-all" monster.

"We could do a couple of broadways and then your guy goes over in the third match or something," Curt suggested, trying to clasp any shred of negotiation.

Danno again shook his head. He had no interest in his guy doing a broadway, or a time-limit draw. "Babu is going to be undefeated and dominant until it's time for us to hand the belt to someone else."

"To who?" Curt asked.

Curt was beginning to get agitated. He had taken down Merv Schiller, the main impediment to Danno's run, and he was starting to get the sense that he was about to get nothing for it.

"I can't say. Not yet," Danno replied.

"You're trying to tell me that you're willing to leave a mountain of money on the table because you're tied up with someone else?"

Now it was Danno's turn to be annoyed. "Listen, Curt. I can't be any clearer than this. I will send the champ to you. He's not losing. He's not going to look weak to an old, broken-down guy like Montrose. My guy is the future. If you want him to come to your territory, you better have something more interesting than a squash match against a washed-up has-been."

Danno's reply had a calming, sobering effect on Curt. "I have been stupid here today, Danno," he said. "This isn't my normal style. I know you're only finding your feet." Curt put out his hand. "Of course we can do business. We'll think of something else. Something better."

Both men shook hands but never took their eyes off each other for a second.

"I was just about to go in," Shane said as they pulled away from the house.

"No need," Curt replied while checking his mirrors to make sure Danno couldn't see the anger in his face.

"You don't look good, Curt," Shane said.

As Curt pulled from the house and onto the open road, he noticed the black sedan approaching from the other side. He shook the gloom from his face, smiled, and tipped his hat as the car passed. Lenny, the driver, acknowledged him in return. The car's passenger, Danno's wife Annie, was reading a paper and didn't notice the gesture.

Curt and Annie Garland would cross paths in the future in a small hotel in Texas.

Shane covered his face as Annie's car passed. Curt noticed.

"You going to fucking tell me or not?" Shane asked.

"He didn't go for it . . ."

Shane threw his hands up in frustration. "I don't fucking believe this man."

"He's not going for it yet. He wanted to do a meaningless thing where the giant comes to Dallas and pins you clean and leaves."

"Fuck no."

"Exactly."

The reality of the situation began to dawn on Shane. "I just moved my family again. Because you told me—"

Curt put a prepared envelope into Shane's lap. "I'm not like the other bosses. There's your first week's payoff."

Shane looked inside. "We didn't shake on payoffs. We shook on me being a partner in this deal."

"Okay, partner," Curt said. "We made no money this week, would you prefer to split that with me fifty-fifty?"

Shane shook his head.

Curt continued. "I'll get this done. Meantime, that's some nice money in there."

Curt was right. The payoff looked thick, and as usual, Shane could sure use the money.

"I'm going to do a trade with Jose Rios," Curt said.

"In Mexico?"

Curt turned into a gas station. They were low. "Yeah, I'm going to get his top star to come to us for a program and then you go down there and return the favor. You hungry?"

Curt opened his door but Shane grabbed his arm. "This isn't what we shook on. We shook on the heavyweight championship, not some guy coming up from Mexico."

"I can't make Danno pick us. We'll have to bide our time. While we're waiting, do you know how much we can make with a Mexican in Dallas?"

Shane wasn't happy but he knew the right Mexican name could draw big money. Not NWC champion money, but enough to live on for a couple of months. "I want a Mexican Mexican. Not a Puerto Rican Mexican. I can't draw money against a Puerto Rican," Shane said.

"Okay. Now, can I get some gas?" Curt asked.

Shane wanted Curt to look him in the face. He wanted Curt to know that he wasn't to be messed with. Not this time. Not again. He said, "I've had enough of being screwed around by you guys. If you try and fuck me over on this deal I will kill you."

Curt nodded. "We're going to make what I said we were going to make."

Shane backed off; his point was made and received. Curt patted down his pockets.

"Fuck," Curt said as he reached into Shane's open envelope. "I'll pay you back when we hit home."

Curt left the car and whistled as he walked to the kiosk. He didn't want to whistle, didn't feel like whistling. But he whistled. Whistling made the broken deal with Danno seem like no big deal.

But Curt knew he was in trouble.

There were boxes and bags and half-opened drawers. A TV sitting atop a makeshift stand of suitcases stacked one on the other. Danno and Annie eating from paper plates, across from each other. Just two people in a home made for more. A lot more.

Danno thought of all the shit he had to crawl through, all the decisions he didn't want to make. He wondered if she still loved him. He watched her watching TV. The smile on her face as she kept full contact with Debbie Reynolds. The way she leaned into her plate, with her food waiting on the fork until she stopped laughing.

Every now and then she'd flick her eyes over to him and smile— not waiting for him to return the gesture. She was happy. The real kind of happy, too. The kind where a person feels content.

A simple night, with a simple meal, in a cobbled-together setting in the middle of a huge, unpacked mansion.

Danno had finally gotten the power and the money. But he knew he was losing her. Her, who he was sure he still loved, who he was sure he couldn't talk to. Who he was sure was having an affair.

He wanted to be angry. He wanted to be a man. More of a man. But he couldn't. He couldn't because he understood it. He could see the reasons why his wife, his rational, kind and loving wife, would cheat on him.

"Cheat" was such a harsh word.

He was a young man when he married her. He promised her children and a certain type of life. She was shy and wanted nothing too explosive. They would talk endlessly about the life they were going to have and the plans they wanted to make. But when they were man and wife, he bounced them around from city to city and became more silent. Less inclusive.

She had begged him not to get into the wrestling business; to stay outside with her and be someone other than his father.

Danno didn't listen. His younger head was far thicker. He had his beautiful wife with him and he found it frustratingly impossible to talk to her. He had wanted to say things to her. Had wanted to apologize for what he had become. Had wanted to wipe it all away and start again.

He wanted to tell her that he loved her.

And all the years passed by and he didn't talk to her. He didn't find a way. He didn't explain to her why he alone made the decisions that shaped her life. She never got what she wanted. Not even half, which would have been at least fair in Danno's mind.

He wanted her to be happy. And he wanted her to be with him. He wanted her to be happy and with him. But one didn't equal the other.

He knew why. It wasn't some mystical edict from the gods. It was him. It was his inability to explain, to confide in his wife. To tell her what made him afraid.

He planned with her, he married her, and then he froze her out.

And still she could be happy as she was, sitting across from him. She was happy. They were not.

Danno stood up and walked around his wife to the door. Their new house was otherwise dark. The fire wasn't lit but the light from the TV made the room look warm. He stood behind her and he wanted to lean in and kiss the top of her head. He wanted to say sorry. He wanted to ask her to stop.

He wanted to, but he didn't do any of those things.

April 2, 1970.
Two years before Annie's murder.
Dallas.

The Sportitorium was a white, barn-like venue that sat on the grounds of Industrial Boulevard. At one time it was one of the whistle-stop spots for blooding new up-and-coming recording artists before they became music megastars.

It was also Curt Magee's base.

Attendance had dropped hugely since those heady days of Johnny Cash and Elvis Presley singing in the center of a rope-less ring, but Curt felt they were on the verge of something. He could feel in his bones that things were close to big time again if he could just hang on. Hang on and make the match—Shane Montrose versus Danno's champion in New York.

"What the fuck is that?" Shane asked as he stepped out of his chauffeured ride into the merciless sun.

"That's Nelly," Curt answered as he walked out of his office to meet him.

"Nelly?" Shane asked, looking at the black bear tied to a tree. "You guys have a bear called Nelly?"

Curt nodded and seemed to want to move quickly into the building and on to other matters.

"That's not for me, is it?" Shane asked, half laughing, half serious.

"We've got something for everyone tonight," Curt said. "I got a bear, some midgets, a few nice ladies, and a gimmick match."

Wrestling fans loved the gimmick matches. They were the matches where the conventional rules of wrestling went out the window. There was the Bullrope Match, where two wrestlers were attached by the wrist to a long rope that had a cowbell in the middle, which could be used as a blunt weapon. Or the Texas Bunkhouse Brawl, which was a free-for-all type match that typically left the arena torn up and the wrestlers drenched in each other's blood.

Tonight, Curt had booked a tar-and-feather match.

Shane was wondering if he'd just landed on another planet. "So, what am I doing?"

"There's a horse," Curt answered.

"I'm wrestling a fucking horse?"

Curt opened the door to the arena and motioned for Shane to follow him inside. "No, you're not wrestling a horse. You're going to
ride one down to the ring for your match later. I figured it would be
a great way to introduce you to the fans here on your first night in.
Give things a little local flavor."

Shane stopped dead in his tracks.

"What's the matter?" Curt asked.

Shane got a strong feeling that he was in the wrong place. He
turned around and could see a scared teenage boy with ginger hair
leaving an open bottle of beer within range of Nelly the bear.

"Go easy on me later, you hear?" the boy said to the bear from a
safe distance.

Nelly had just met her "opponent" for that night.

Curt walked around Shane and into his line of sight. "What's the
matter?" Curt asked again.

"I ain't no cowboy," Shane said softly.

Curt had spent all he had on this show. He had even sold his
car to pay for the animals. He needed his number-one draw to be
happy. "We need to get you over with the audience. We need you
to go out there and get them on your side the second they see you,"
Curt explained.

Shane couldn't have been more insulted. For any owner to tell an
old pro like Shane Montrose how to get over with an audience was a
slap in the face. Like telling a virtuoso how to play the piano.

"Have you ever seen me in the ring?" Shane asked.

"Of course I have. But down here it's different. Trust me," Curt
answered.

"I've wrestled down south for most of my career. I know all about
the southern fans."

Curt smiled. "You're not in the South no more, Shane. You're in
Texas now, boy."

CHAPTER SEVEN

October 10, 1972.
Four days after Annie's murder.
Nevada.

Bree boarded her number nine bus. Her hastily packed suitcase was jammed tightly against her knees and the seat in front. The case had already been dragged across the country and shoved in a motel wardrobe, only to be packed and dragged away again. Bree was heading to Bakersfield not really knowing what to expect. She just knew she wanted to see her father. Outside the bus window, her sons waved goodbye as she took off along the hot and dusty road. Her stomach turned at the thoughts of them staying behind without her. It also turned a little at the thought of Lenny being solely responsible for their collective well-being.

"Goodbye," she mouthed through the grubby window. "I love you."

Lenny's back was turned to the bus as he made a call at the station's pay phone. Bree wondered what he was doing. Luke waved frantically; it was the first time in his young life that he was going to be away from his mother. He didn't really want to be left there at all.

"We're going to fly into New York today, Mom," Lenny said on the phone as his wife's bus pulled away. "Can you mind the boys?"

"Me and your father won't be here, Lenard. We're going to head on down to your aunt Hendy's birthday party," Lenny's mother replied.

Lenny paused for a second to think.

"Why don't you bring the little ones there?" his mother asked.

"Can I?" Lenny asked.

Luke tugged on his father's shirt as Bree's bus disappeared out onto the road.

Bree was desperate to get Lenny's attention before she pulled off on her journey. She was waving like crazy and blowing kisses to her boys as her bus began to turn.

"Dad?" Luke said, trying to get Lenny to look.

Lenny just shrugged him off and continued talking to his mother.

She said, "You can come down to the Hendys' with them but I don't want you dropping them down there."

"Why not?" Lenny asked.

"Because your father and I want to have some cocktails and stay for a few days. Do you know how long it's been since we've been on vacation?"

Bree's bus was out of sight before Lenny realized his opportunity to say goodbye was long gone. *Fuck.*

"You can stay at home. I'll leave you guys dinners and things. Your father is telling me to tell you that you're not to touch his car," Lenny's mother said.

"I won't."

"He loves that car, Lenard."

"I know."

"What are you coming back so soon for anyways?"

A couple of years before, Danno had given Lenny a few grand here and there to stockpile in Lenny's shed. It was a strategy that all the bosses used just in case they needed to get out of town in a hurry. They had money stashed everywhere. Everywhere but a bank.

Danno showing such faith in Lenny had Lenny feeling like one of the inner circle. He was only too happy to take on the job. Not that he could tell his wife what he was doing.

"Lenard?"

Lenny was staring at the hill in the road. He wished Bree's bus would come back so he could say goodbye to her.

"Lenard?" Lenny's mother shouted again through the phone.

"What?" he answered.

"What are you coming back to town so quickly for?" she asked him.

"I'm just coming back to collect something for someone. I'll just be a day or two."

Lenny had found Danno's money underneath the wardrobe in his motel room. Now he wanted his wife's rings back.

Nestor took a second to figure out just how he was going to approach his loaded hotdog. Every day he went to the same cart on the same corner, and every day he came away with a dog too full to eat with any semblance of grace.

Fuck it. That's what napkins are for.

As soon as he bit down and his mouth was full, he saw Captain Miller approaching from across the street. This cart wasn't close to their precinct. Nestor picked it for that one feature. "Good?" Miller asked.

Nestor could only nod, mumble, and wipe his mouth.

"I'll have whatever he had," Miller said to the guy behind the cart.

Nestor chewed as fast as he could. He swallowed way too soon and the lump of food burned his throat on the way down.

Miller muttered under his breath, "Any more on Garland?"

Nestor shook his head and licked his fingers. "I don't think he's our guy."

"No?"

Nestor shook his head again. "From what I see. No."

Captain Miller turned back to the cart to pick his sauces and hand the guy his money. He began to walk slowly away and Nestor followed.

"I've got this guy, this Melvin Pritchard for the State Athletic Commission, who is *convinced* Garland has something to do with this."

"He thinks Garland did this?"

"I don't think he means that Garland actually took a knife to the senator. But he does think that Garland was behind it."

"Huh," Nestor said as he took another bite.

"Anything from your side with Garland's dirty lawyer?" the captain asked.

"I'm working on it. Nothing so far."

Captain Miller stopped. "OK. You keep me posted."

Nestor nodded and chewed his way through another oversized bite as he watched Miller dump his dog whole in the trash and walk back across the street.

The captain wasn't there to eat.

Pennsylvania.

The Philadelphia Arena wasn't Madison Square Garden by any stretch of the imagination. It was a dingy and dark hardwood-floor venue used for everything from college basketball to rodeo. But it would be full. Unlike the Garden. It still had the painted white brick dressing room. The wooden benches. The chewing tobacco. The cards. The beers. The smoke. The ball breaking. Like nearly every other venue.

Backstage, two wrestlers were standing in their underwear, washing their ring trunks in the sink after fifteen days on the road. Everyone else "washed" by splashing a generous amount of Brut in delicate areas. A huge three-hundred-pound powerlifter was putting on his flowery shower cap to spare his newly dyed locks from the water.

Huge, scary men, getting ready for their audience.

Their bags were pungent, something their huge hangovers could do without. Some broke away from the card game to warm up in the corner. Another broke away to puke up the previous night's adventures. These men were sore, beat-up, tired, hungover, homesick—and ready to go again. Same as they were last week, last month, last year. The show was never over for wrestlers.

Even when they got to occasionally go home, they were still "on" and in character. Any interviews or media appearances, any time they left their home—they were who you saw on TV. They went by their wrestler names and acted like their wrestling personas—everywhere. Some of the Boys even stayed that way around their own families, 24/7. Protect the business at all costs. They all knew the money was in making people believe. And some of the Boys didn't trust their wives and their big mouths to keep the con quiet.

Children grew up thinking their fathers were getting beaten every week on TV, wives thought their husbands were as rich and as flashy as their cocky character appeared to be. Wrestling and being a wrestler was an always-on, never-stop profession. The situation inevitably led to breakdowns and mounting pressure.

Outside, Ricky hurried through the door. He needed to tape enough matches for a few weeks of TV and get the wrestlers to cut interviews for the different markets the matches would be shown in. Babu was on his mind too. Ricky had an idea that could see the seven-foot, four-hundred-pound giant get his heat back in New York—become the most despised wrestler in the country again. In wrestling, you worked hard to get your customers to hate you. That way they paid to see you get your ass kicked by someone they loved. The beautiful con in wrestling was that the company "owned" both the person you loved and the person you hated, so either way it got all of your money.

Ricky needed to get all this done and then shoot back to New York to meet the other bosses at midnight. He had been around a long time, had seen a lot of things within the NWC, so he knew this bad feeling between them and Danno was about to spill over into something really bad.

New York.

Danno stood outside a building with his finger pressed on the buzzer with no number.

"Fucking . . . stupid . . . fuck," Danno mumbled to himself as he stood back and looked up at the window. "Troy?" Danno shouted.

Troy Bartlett was Danno's trusted lawyer. He moved paper around, sprung wrestlers from jail, and kept anything illegal out of sight. He was on call all day, every day. Danno never had to wait more than a half hour for him to return a call or make it to his house to discuss business. But now it had been days since he'd last heard from him.

Danno stood outside the shitty little uptown office and left his finger on the buzzer once more. He thought he was in the right place. All their previous business was conducted at Danno's place or on the road.

There was nothing. No answer, and it was getting late.

What the fuck is going on?

"Mr. Garland?" a cautious voice asked from behind.

Danno turned to see a slight, nervous-looking young woman getting out from a parked car. He didn't answer her. The young woman took a look around and walked closer to Danno. "Did you get my note?"

Danno watched her very carefully. "Who are you?"

The young woman was unsure of how much she could say on the street. "I left a note for you." She waited for Danno to give her a sign that he knew what she was talking about. He didn't.

"I asked you who you were," Danno said.

"I'm sorry. I'm Katy. Spence. I work here. We've never . . ."

Katy could see that Danno was clamming up. He didn't look too impressed with her explanation so far. "I can let you in to see for yourself," she said as she fished out a bunch of keys from her purse and opened the office door.

"That's fine," Danno said, softening a little.

Katy said, "Troy . . . Mr. Bartlett . . . left two days ago and I haven't seen him since."

"He left. For where?"

"He said he had to get away for a while," she said nervously.

"Get away from what?" Danno asked.

Katy was reluctant to answer, but she knew she had no choice. "You, sir. He said he had to get away from you."

Danno and Katy sat opposite each other in the diner across from the office. It was busy and loud. Waitresses glided around with plates and coffee pots as patrons struggled to catch their eye. Usually Danno would eat half the menu and sample the other half. Today, he wasn't in the mood. The car that had been parked right outside the diner since they had gotten there wasn't helping, either.

Katy wiped the spilled coffee from her chin and Danno handed her another napkin.

"You seem very nervous," Danno said.

"I'm not cut out for this," she replied with the weight of honesty. "He frightened me with the way he was talking. He was paranoid and jumpy. Pacing around and biting his nails. Now, even when I'm in my own home I'm pulling the drapes closed in the day, and I don't know why."

Danno wanted to see just who this woman was. "Why don't you write out that note for me now?"

"It just said—"

Danno stopped her. "I'd prefer if you'd write it down."

Katy nervously reached into her bag and took out a notepad and pen. Danno wanted to make sure her writing matched the note that was left under his door. As soon as she began to write Danno could see that it was indeed her handwriting on the note he had.

Danno slapped the table. "Could he not just have called me?"

The diner quieted down and looked over to Danno's table. Katy was clearly uncomfortable with the aggression. Danno caught himself and toned it down.

"Notes. And sneaking around. I mean . . . call me," Danno said in a much more reasonable voice.

She stammered, "Pardon my . . . I don't know what to call it. My . . . forwardness. And I love Mr. Bartlett . . . but he wasn't thinking much about anything or anyone beside himself. He just said that they were coming for you. That's all."

Danno leaned in. "Who's coming for me?"

"The police," she replied.

Both Danno and Katy leaned back from their conversation as the waitress put their bill on the table and left again. Katy opened her purse and rummaged around for some money. Danno could see that she hadn't got much. She was like his wrestlers. No work. No pay.

She continued as she foraged. "He said that I should tell you to wrap all the loose ends up. Cover your tracks. Smooth over whatever it is you need to before the cops . . . you know . . . arrive."

Danno put on his tweed cap. "If he contacts you for anything, you make sure and get him to call me. You hear me?"

Katy nodded and pushed her coffee cup into the middle of the table with a slightly trembling hand. Her red hair reminded Danno of something. Something nice. Something good. But his attention was pulled away from that nice thought to whoever it was that was sitting in the parked car across the street.

"Did he leave you anything?" he asked. "Any money, I mean."

"I'm fine. Thank you."

Danno opened up a folded stack of notes that were held in place by an engraved money clip and ripped out a tidy bundle.

"No, I can't," Katy said, embarrassed.

"We don't know how long he'll be gone for, Miss. Take this to tide you over," Danno said as he put the money on the table. He was insistent but kind.

"Thank you," she said unable to look Danno in the eye.

"You should have all of this," he said as he reconsidered and left her the full clip of money.

Katy instinctively rose out of her seat. "No, no. I can't. Thank you though."

Danno left without hearing her argument. He wanted to pay the driver across the street a visit.

Pennsylvania.

Ricky sat alone, going over the card for the next night. He knew the payoffs for the Boys were going to be rough in New York. They had all been promised more after Danno got control of San Francisco and Florida. This was supposed to be the start of the super payoffs— feuds and matches that could crisscross the country. But it was all falling apart.

Danno wanted New York, Florida, San Francisco, and Texas. And he had gotten most of them. But now they were, de facto, Ricky's problem. He couldn't let such huge territories die on the vine, but he didn't have the authority to execute any major plan on his own. He was trapped. He could neither retreat nor advance. Nor could he depend on his boss for a game plan.

The hall outside was packed with wrestlers who were full of questions and problems. Ricky didn't want to talk to any of them. He only had one meeting on his mind. Not the type of meeting that he wanted to have, but one that he had to have. He needed Danno's direction.

"We need to talk," Oscar Dewsbury said as he pushed into Ricky's locker room uninvited. "What is this shit, man?"

Ricky waited silently for him to get to the point.

"They're telling me that I'm suspended. That fucking asshole from the Athletic Commission is saying that I no-showed a match in Fresno two nights ago."

Not so long before, Oscar Dewsbury had left Danno Garland high and dry when he jumped from New York to the rival Florida territory. Unfortunately for him, Danno eventually got control of Florida—and Oscar Dewsbury was once again on his books. Danno never forgot who fucked him over. Never forgave either. On the night he took over Florida, before he had heard his wife was murdered, Danno Garland had looked to even things up a bit with Oscar.

Oscar continued, "I have to pay a five-hundred-dollar fine too. How the fuck am I supposed to eat?"

Ricky snapped from his deeper thoughts and drew a breath. "If you no-show, they do what they do. Take it up with them."

"I was in Tampa that night. Working. You fucking booked me to go there. Danno knows that. That's why he booked me in two towns and didn't tell me. Isn't it? He knew what he was doing. That fucking—"

Ricky quickly grabbed his massive visitor by the neck and slammed him against the cold wall. "You think with everything he has going on in his life right now that he took the time to fuck with you? You're lucky he's as lenient as he is. The way you screwed him over. Who leaves a man when he's down? Hah? You took the money and ran when things were tight up here. I would shut my mouth if I were you. Do you hear me?"

Oscar could feel Ricky's grip bending his windpipe and closing off his carotid artery. He could only nod.

Ricky released him but wanted to follow up with a head-butt to punctuate his point. "You fucking respect that man and everything that's going on for him right now," Ricky said of his boss.

Oscar rubbed his throat and tried swallowing normally.

"Now get the fuck out of here," Ricky said.

Oscar stumbled out the door and Ricky stood in the middle of the room. He had to roll the dice. He had to come up with something outside of the everyday. Ricky knew that if he didn't propose something to keep the other bosses happy, then Danno was a sitting duck.

New York.

"Who the fuck are you?" Danno asked as he approached the car across from the diner. The daylight was gone and the figure looked a little more mysterious sitting there in half-light with his window open.

Behind Danno, Katy ran from the diner with her purse full of his money.

"I'm a cop," the man in the driver's seat replied. "My name is Nestor. Why don't you hop in here?"

Danno smirked.

"I'm on break," Nestor said as he showed Danno his Thermos and homemade sandwiches.

"Fuck you," Danno answered and walked the other way.

"You don't look so good, Mr. Garland. Are you looking after yourself since . . . you know, Mrs. Garland?"

Nestor opened his car door and stood on the street.

"What's your deal?" Danno asked as he turned back around.

Nestor answered quickly, "I'm a friend of a friend of yours."

Danno was just trying to figure out if his new admirer was being helpful to be helpful, or being helpful to get information.

"And who would that be?" Danno asked.

"Why don't you get in so I don't have to do this on the street?" Nestor said.

"Are you arresting me?" Danno asked.

"I'm offering you a sandwich."

Nestor could see Danno thinking about it. "I can't promise the bread is too fresh is all," Nestor said. "Coffee is good, though."

He could see the doubt in Danno's face. Nestor suddenly realized how stupid it was to ask Danno to get in a car with a stranger, so he showed him his badge and his most trustworthy face.

"You're going to have to trust me here for a couple of minutes, Danno," Nestor said as he drove.

"You won't be offended if I don't," Danno answered.

Nestor enjoyed Danno's response. "No, I don't suppose I will."

"What do you want?" Danno asked as they cruised down Empire Boulevard.

"I don't give a fuck if you make your money from throwing matches. It's not on my list of the shittiest crimes in this city."

"One of my guys would handle your whole boxing club," Danno replied, deeply offended.

"All right, old man. Whatever you say. I'm just saying. I don't want nothing from you. I'm not looking for you to tell me anything, tip me off, or anything else."

"Who's your friend that's my friend?" Danno asked after a slight pause.

"Let's just say that your legal counsel asked me to touch base with you," Nestor replied.

Danno wasn't impressed. "Everyone knows I use Troy Bartlett as my counsel."

"Troy who? I have no idea who you're talking about," Nestor replied with a smile. He lit up a cigarette and rolled down the window. "You need to start worrying about your own ass."

"And why's that?" Danno asked.

Nestor shook his head. "A US senator gets stabbed on a New York street and a whole lot of lazy, fat captains and police chiefs suddenly get motivated. You were sloppy, Danno."

"I had nothing to do with it," he truthfully replied.

Nestor turned his gaze straight ahead and packaged his next sentence as softly as he could. "They have one of your guys who says he'll talk."

Danno's stomach sank.

"He's coming in soon. Sounds like tomorrow night," Nestor continued.

Danno didn't react in the slightest. He didn't want to give the stranger beside him any inkling of what he might be thinking or feeling.

Nestor stopped at a traffic light. "I don't know who your rat is yet. So far only the higher-ups have a name."

Danno took a sandwich to try to show how little of a fuck he gave about the news he was hearing. "Let whoever it is come in and waste your time. I have nothing worth talking about," Danno said as he opened his car door. "And if any of you fucking people want to arrest me, then you come see me. Until then . . ."

Danno slammed the door and began to walk. Nestor pulled up tight to Danno on the sidewalk and softly said, "When this guy comes and opens his mouth, your room to maneuver is gone. If you have anything that you need to clean up or hide away, now is the time."

CHAPTER EIGHT

September 28, 1970.
Two years before Annie's murder.
Texas.

"What fucking else even makes sense?" Shane asked the stoic bearded man who was sitting opposite him. The Sugarstick was completely naked in the otherwise empty locker room and had a long white line, chopped into perfection, in front of him.

"What's your name?" Shane asked.

"Bert."

Shane laughed. "Bert?"

"Yeah, Bert," Bert replied.

"You don't look like a Bert."

"Well, I am a Bert."

"Okay, Bert."

Shane swooped down and snorted his line and continued his stream of thoughts. "You see Babu is across the ring from me and the arena is full. I bump all over him, making him look like a fucking brick wall. He shines me up. Boom. Boom. Kicking my ass. The girls are screaming . . . I fucking slide to the corner with my hands up to heaven. He smiles like he knows I can't take anymore and then I give him the 'fuck you' face and drag myself on the ground to fight again. He's got me by my tights and *whack*, fucking head-butts me in my chest . . ." Sugarstick broke to snort his line. "I fall down like a puppet without strings. The place goes crazy and starts chanting my name."

Shane jumped and began to "see" it play out in front of him. He noticed the expressionless face across from him, but continued regardless. "And then he makes a mistake. And I slowly fire everything I have at him. Wham. I hit him in the throat with a closed fist. I hide it from the ref but the people forgive me for cheating a little. I fucking chop-block his tree trunk leg and he starts to wobble. And that big giant fuck is good at selling those, too. He'll make it look like it's the first time in the world that he's ever been hit that hard before. And man, I start to feel it. I start to feel the people running through my veins. I hit the ropes and fucking whack that big fuck across the throat with a clothesline. I mean stick it to him. And he starts to wave his arms like he's trying everything he can just to stay standing and I run and hit those motherfucking ropes again and fucking *ba-bam* him across the throat again. The people can see he's going and they will me to hit him one last time. Take this big fucker off his feet for the first time in his life. The giant is in shock. Never happened before. And I hit the ropes as hard and as fast as I can and . . . *spadoink* . . . he catches me in the fucking chin with a big boot and I go down like someone in the nosebleed seats just fucking shot me." Sugarstick lay prostrate on the floor.

"And I'm lying on my chest hiding my face and I'm thinking, I fucking got you, man. I got you fucking marks in the audience to cheer and believe that I could win this time, and you fucking backed me, and I got a fucking boot in the fucking face so fuck you. Miracles don't happen and giants don't fucking get taken off their feet. Until the next time I make a comeback and make you think the same thing again. That's my job, you see? I get them to pay money to see me win. And then fuck them. Huh? And I go to the next town and do it all again."

Bert stood up and slid a small brown bag along the dressing room bench. "That's thirty-seven thousand owed in total. Payments go up accordingly plus twenty points," he said as he lumbered toward the door.

"That's no problem," Shane replied, almost offended at the subject of money at all.

"I'll be back to collect."

"No problem, I said," Shane replied, even more offended now that he mentioned the money again.

"If you don't pay, I break the small finger on each hand *and* double the repayments for twice as long. You understand?" Bert asked.

Shane felt the need to cover himself up now. The atmosphere wasn't a pleasant place for his penis to be hanging out.

"What did you think of my match idea with Babu?" Shane asked.

"I don't care. It's fake." Bert turned to leave but Shane rushed him.

"Fake?" Shane asked as he launched himself onto Bert's back.

Bert pulled Shane off of his back with ease and slapped some sense into him with two open-handed wallops. There was a sobering pause. "You come at me again and I kill you," Bert warned.

Shane—naked, humbled, and vulnerable—could only nod. "Okay."

Outside the venue Bert shook his head as he saw all the fans lining up at the entrance to the venue. He couldn't understand in the slightest why people would want to pay money to see this wrestling shit. He opened his car door and sat in his seat before getting hit across the side of his face with an old oak table leg.

Shane Montrose, still naked, still coked out of his mind, beat away on the guy who called his sport "fake," with fists and knees and the table leg over and over until there was blood and broken bones. Some staff managed to come out to stop him.

"You'll get your money when I say so. You fucking owe me money now. How about that, Bert? That's right. You owe me a million fucking dollars now. I'll collect it tomorrow."

Shane was bundled back into the building before anyone in line could make out their naked, high, main-event star beating a guy called Bert with the leg of a table.

Shane sat in the front bleacher with ice strapped to his knees and both shoulders. He was sweaty and too tired to move from the seat. The Sportitorium was empty and covered in trash after a raucous night of wrestling action. Shane smoked, not in any rush to get home.

"Hey," Curt said as he entered through the tunnel.

"We need a new ring. That one is covered in mildew. And it's like a rock," Shane said.

Curt hovered but said nothing.

"What was the house?" Shane asked.

"It was better. Looking like nearly a thousand paid."

Curt sat down in the seat next to Shane.

"That's still terrible," Shane said. "I'm working my ass off out there. I want an ass every eighteen inches. No empty seats."

"What happened outside earlier?" Curt asked. "One of the Boys said they seen you nearly kill a guy out there."

"It was nothing. Personal matter," Shane replied. "Doesn't matter. All that matters is the size of the house. The money we're pulling in."

"The house here is slightly better, but TV . . . there's a problem."

Curt's words got Shane's fullest attention. The wrestler knew that having local TV was the biggest marketing tool the wrestling business had. Any trouble on the TV side of the business meant trouble across the business as a whole.

"What's wrong with TV?" Shane asked.

Curt was clearly worn out. "There's some internal dispute at the station. Something about ownership. Nothing to do with us," Curt said.

Shane could smell bullshit. "What dispute?"

"They're not really saying." Curt lit up a smoke of his own. He rubbed his tired eyes and wondered what was keeping him in this business at all. "They seem okay with not collecting our money every month," Curt said shaking his head.

"If we got no TV then we're finished," Shane said as he turned directly to his partner.

"Now, we're not done yet."

Shane tore the tape from his icepacks and let them fall on the floor. He picked up his bag and heaved it toward the ring in frustration. "What's really going on here?" Shane demanded.

Curt took a second before answering. He wasn't used to talking to wrestlers like this, but Shane needed to know what was on his mind. "I think it might be Danno Garland."

"What?" Shane asked.

"I think he might be paying the station here to keep us off the air."

"He's paying them to *not* have us on air?" Shane asked.

Curt nodded. "I think so. Looks like he's trying to starve us down here."

"Why the fuck would he do that?"

Curt in turn stood up and looked his partner in the face. "I have no idea. It seems he really don't like one of us for some unknown reason."

October 10, 1972.
Four days after Annie's murder.
New York.

Ricky returned and took the steps into the shitty back room where Annie's wake had been held earlier that day. He wasn't surprised this was where the bosses chose to meet. The greedy fucks probably got a special daily rate on the place.

There was always an angle with the bosses.

He opened the door slowly and watched the dark sides of the room with great interest as he walked toward the table of bosses at the top of the room.

"Gentlemen," Ricky said as he approached along the sticky floor.

Most of the bosses were still huddled in the corner. All the wrestlers were gone. There was only a circle of Scotch, chewing tobacco, and cigar smoke left.

"Where's Danno?" Tanner Blackwell asked.

"I'm here," Ricky replied.

His response seemed to anger some in the circle. A few of the bosses threw their hands in the air in exasperation and sighed their disapproval.

Ricky knew he needed to pull the bosses back into the conversation quickly. "I'm speaking with Danno's full permission and on his behalf. I don't think it's unreasonable to give the man some more time to grieve."

"Thanks to all the shit you guys are pulling up here, we don't fucking have time for grieving," Tanner shouted. "The walls are moving in on us fast."

Joe Lapine spoke softly from the head of the table. "Give the man a chance to speak."

The circle widened out and the bosses sat shoulder to shoulder in silence and waited for Ricky to begin.

"I need your help," Ricky said.

Tanner smiled at the predicament Danno, through Ricky, found himself in. One week before, Danno had looked immovable as the top man, now his number two was at the meeting looking for their help.

How quickly things can change.

"What are you asking for Ricky?" Joe asked. "What's your proposal?"

Ricky continued. "I want to open out the Garden to your guys tomorrow night. I want to run an elite tournament that would put all of our top guys in there. Proctor has run off somewhere—afraid to face the giant. We strip him of the title . . ."

Tanner again chimed in. "What the fuck does that do for us?"

Ricky wanted to launch himself across the table and beat Tanner's face in. He steadied himself and continued. "We take a new path. One with more room and more money. We tape this tournament at the Garden tomorrow. Then we all use the same footage on our local TVs. All your guys will look like a million dollars fighting for the biggest prize in wrestling, in the most prestigious venue in wrestling. We'll make your guys look like stars."

"But there can be only one winner, Ricky," Joe pointed out.

Joe's point had some nodding along in agreement.

Ricky shook his head. "No. Two."

"Two? How the fuck can two win?" Tanner asked.

Ricky continued. "In the main event we have a double pinfall. Both wrestlers' shoulders on the mat at the same time when the referee counts to three. We have chaos and both men leave claiming the title of Heavyweight Champion of World. One for us here in New York. And one for whoever you guys decide. Then both men crisscross the whole country for six months calling themselves champion. Never a day off. Two matches on Saturdays and two on Sundays."

With every word, Ricky could feel the room moving his way. The body language was different. The hecklers silenced. Ricky could see that his proposal was sinking in well with most of them.

He continued, "We all get twice the money that one champion can bring us. We all work together to get our business back on track, and we all make good out of it. Then at the end of six months, when all of this calms down, we put the two champions together and sell a super-bout for the ages. Two world champions clashing to decide who is the real world champion."

Joe tried to read the room from the side of his eye. He thought that Ricky might just have found a perfect win/win scenario to put his members at ease. All but one.

"Why six months?" Tanner asked.

Ricky replied, "Because I want Danno to have the say in who ulti-mately wins and claims the unified title again. It's his belt to hand over if he wants. Or to keep if he wants. I just want him to have time to come back to the table."

Silence. But a good silence. Joe stood up from the gathering and walked toward Ricky.

"Thanks," Joe said as he escorted Ricky to the door.

Tanner stood too. "Wait."

Ricky and Joe stopped and turned around.

"What about Danno putting out a bounty on Curt Magee?" Tanner asked. "Not in the history of our great business have I ever heard of such a fucked-up move from one boss to another."

"We can't have that," Joe said in support of Tanner's question.

"I'll talk to him," Ricky said.

"Talk to him?" Tanner asked.

Ricky nodded.

Tanner wasn't at all happy with Ricky's soft approach. "No. You fucking tell him that if he does anything else to draw attention to this business then all the talking stops. And I don't mind singling myself out here, Ricky, as the one who will stop it."

Ricky studied the room to see if the rest of the bosses thought that Tanner's threat was out of line. Apparently, it wasn't.

"I understand," Ricky said as he turned back for the door.

Joe walked with him through the door. Both men stopped at the top of the stairs, out of earshot.

"Where does Danno want the other champion to come from?" Joe asked.

"Tanner," Ricky quickly answered.

"Tanner?" Joe asked.

Ricky nodded his head. "Yeah, Tanner is giving up Curt."

Even Joe, who had seen it all, was stunned. "What?"

Ricky buttoned up his coat. "For all his bullshit, Tanner is taking the bounty on Curt. He's meeting Danno tomorrow to give up Curt's whereabouts and to collect the cash. So Danno wants him to have the second champion."

"Alright," Joe said, well aware of his duty.

Ricky put out his hand. "We need to get this going now. I have everything lined up at the Garden. I hope you can get this done."

"Me too," Joe replied unconvincingly.

Both men shook hands and both men went to work.

Across town, wrestlers were getting fucked up. Two hours before and the music pouring from the speakers would have made the troop of wrestlers on the dance floor more than likely to kill someone. Now, knee deep into the "wake," they were drunk, stoned, horny, and on a night off.

"Just the way Annie Garland would have wanted it," one of them noted sarcastically.

They were also heels. Bad guys. Not liked. The babyfaces went to a different club.

The Sugarstick, Shane Montrose, was a "tweener." A bad guy in New York and a babyface in Texas. He was so good at his job that even the most ardent fans bought him drinks out of pure respect.

And he drank them. Every single one.

He also threw fistfuls of money into the air and watched all the women around him dive to their knees in an effort to scrape some bills from the floor. He laughed as they pulled at each other's hair and ripped at each other's clothes. He danced without any semblance of style, control, or grace in the middle of the floor. The women were drawn to him and their men were just waiting to test themselves against the visiting "fake" wrestlers. Across the floor, those same wrestlers sat in hope that the men would try and see how "fake" they were. For them, breaking a few jaws would have been the cherry on the cake of a perfect evening. Nothing bonds professional wrestlers like a huge brawl.

The Sugarstick turned and twisted and rubbed himself in unison with the music and the week's worth of drugs in his system. As he floated around he could hardly contain his joy at being alive. The rush of being there, in that room, with those people, listening to that song was overwhelming. His eyes moistened with intense chemical love and joy.

In a world of his own he spoke to himself as his hips operated independently from his mind. From the inside looking out he felt warm and confident and content and happy and at ease and strong and irresistible and forceful and capable and wrapped in all things good. From the outside looking in he looked like a fucking lunatic. An embarrassment. Someone who, without money and wrestling fame, would have been thrown out on his ass a long time ago. He looked like someone who should be at home with his kids or grandkids.

Shane nearly choked on the emotion rising in his throat. He reached out his arms to bathe in the moment. He spun fast enough to blur the room as he turned. He saw a head of jet black, perfectly pressed, long hair on each rotation. He wanted to feel it, to know what it might smell like. So he grabbed onto it as he pivoted clumsily and yanked the woman attached to it from her seat.

"Fucking greatness," he shouted as he pulled the screaming woman around and around with him. Her girlfriends shook the Sugarstick and punched and slapped him to make him let go. This hair he held was great. Soft. Strong. Even though it was attached to someone else, it belonged to him.

As he turned, he was somewhere else. Somewhere where he wasn't the scumbag he knew himself to be. Somewhere where he wasn't crippled with guilt and flashbacks. Somewhere where he was the undefeated world champion.

Shane Montrose lay motionless on the brown carpet. The meager contents of his turquoise hotel room were tossed and tipped over, except the umber-colored bed, which was still perfectly dressed. His window was open and the earth-colored floral curtains flapped in the breeze. On the floor, Shane hugged the phone. Even in his drunken stupor, he begged it to ring. Just ring. For hours he checked the dial tone and rang the front desk to make sure the lines were good. He paid the disgusting concierge richly to monitor the phones all day and all night. But wish though he did, no call came through. He left his hotel phone number everywhere he knew Curt went or might be.

The Hotel Monterey wasn't the usual standard that the Sugarstick liked for himself when he was on the road. But when he left for New York he didn't know if he was going to be there for a night or a week. Either way, he felt he had to be where people wouldn't think to look. Just in case his problems from home fancied a trip to the Big Apple.

Ring, goddamn it.

He impatiently banged some numbers on his phone and waited. A sleepy female voice answered. "Hello?"

"Hey, honey, any messages from home yet?" he said in his fake-sober, chirpy voice.

"Shane?" his wife asked.

"Is your brother still checking our machine because I'm really waiting on an important . . . ?"

"There's no message over there. He's checking."

"Is he going to the house every day? Twice a day?" he asked.

There was a slight confused pause. "What? Yes. He snuck on over there this evening. There's nothing there."

Shane was bewildered. "You sure he's doing what he says he's doing?"

"Yes. I want to go home, Shane. I want to sleep in my own bed."

Shane did all he could to hide his frustration. "Are you sure he knows how to work the answer machine? Curt should have called by now."

She had had enough. "Yes. Blinking red light. He's checking the goddamn machine," his wife shouted back.

Shane couldn't believe his bad fucking luck. Another night without knowing where Curt was. "You've got this number, honey? Haven't you?"

Shane's wife was growing more and more anxious with every question Shane asked her. "You've given it to me twice now. Is there something else wrong?" she asked.

"Go back to sleep," he said as he waited for silence on the other end.

"When are you going to get these people their money? We can't keep doing this. I want . . ."

"I'm trying."

"You're trying what? What are you trying? Your family is hiding in my brother's house because we're too afraid to go home."

"What do you want me to do?" he shouted.

"Fix this," she shouted back. "You. Fix. This."

Shane slammed down the phone repeatedly in anger and frustration.

"I'm fucking trying here," he shouted in his empty room. "I'm trying."

It really came down to two men. Joe Lapine as chairman of NWC and Tanner Blackwell as chief opponent. The National Wrestling Council was made up of many members across the world, but the power to make this decision lay at the top. And now that Danno was weakened and distracted, that power was moving to Joe and Tanner.

The two men faced each other across a small round room-service table in a large hotel room. They were happy to leave the meeting and let their wrestlers spread out across Manhattan to drink and hit the nightclubs. Tanner even gave some of his wrestlers an extra hundred to break a few faces while they were out. It was always a good investment for the bosses to pay their guys a little more to be tough with the locals. It protected the business and made wrestlers the one group of people you didn't want to mess with in a bar. The more people they could prove they were 'legitimate' to, the longer the deception could go on.

Joe and Tanner's plates were filled with steak and vegetables while exotic desserts waited for them in the middle of the table. These were the plates of bosses who were earning money. The hotel room made the same extravagant statement. A room too big and too pricey for the single man staying there. But that was wrestling. A con. A sleight of hand. A play, from the second their eyes opened 'til the second they shut. Everyone in the wrestling business knew they were taking the money from the paying public, the "marks" as they called them. They knew they were conning them. But they also conned each other. It was a con of perception rather than deception. They all did it to each other all the time.

Even the bosses did it. Joe Lapine and Tanner Blackwell sat opposite each other, out-ordering each other with room service. They arrived on separate chartered flights, drove in separate limos, and booked the finest rooms in the finest hotels in New York.

And they were both broke.

Not broke like a guy who sleeps in the alleyway broke. But broke for a rich guy broke. And they knew, like all the other bosses around the world, that Annie Garland's funeral was the place to be seen. They called in favors to borrow expensive jewelry or pawned their second cars for pocket money. If you're not seen *like* a boss then you weren't seen *as* a boss. And to be seen as a boss you had to flaunt. Everything. All the time.

Tanner all of a sudden dropped his cutlery, like he couldn't take it anymore. "I don't know if this is the right time to be seen to be closer to Danno."

Joe wiped the side of his mouth before speaking. "Now is the perfect time to seem closer to Danno."

Tanner had a little think before picking up his fork again. "Why do you say that?"

"There's going to be two champions coming off the card tomorrow night. Danno has got one and you could have one. If something were to go wrong with Danno, who do you think is next in line?"

Tanner couldn't hide his grin. "Why are you so adamant that I have it?"

Joe pushed his plate back completely and cleared the food from his back teeth with his tongue. "Danno has essentially triple the vote when it comes to the title. He has New York, San Francisco, and Florida. We have one vote. We're going to be a long time out in the cold if we don't take this gift now. I've got nobody ready. I'm voting for this. And Danno's three. If you vote too, then it's a done deal that I can present to the members as a *fait accompli*. With that, you get the other title."

Tanner was back to full speed in shoveling his food into his mouth. "If I link myself to Danno and he fucks me over . . ."

"You know what the field is out there at the moment. You just have to decide if it's too hot for you. Let me know and I'll arrange someone else to . . ."

"We should get another bottle of champagne," Tanner said. "To celebrate."

CHAPTER NINE

May 12, 1972.
Five months before Annie's murder.
Texas.

Grobie pulled a chicken from the oven and threw it, along with the shallow pan it sat on, into the sink. "You fucking hot chicken," she said as she sucked on her burned thumb. She scraped the broken carcass from the bottom of the sink and slapped it onto a plate before dumping some half-frozen vegetables around the broken bones.

"Curt?" she shouted through to the front of her tiny, cluttered house. Not getting an answer within two nanoseconds, she shouted the same again—only louder. "Curt."

"Yes. Jesus," Curt Magee replied as he walked into the small kitchen with a beer in his hand. The more his business broke down, the more time he spent sleeping in his mistress's house. Or at least Grobie was his mistress when he was married; now she was his little secret that he hid away. Especially as she was only nineteen and already had a two-year-old son with him.

"Where's your friend?" she asked.

"Don't," he warned her.

"What?" she asked.

"Don't. I fucking see you. Don't."

Curt noticeably slowed down as he came to the window and peeked outside before walking to the table.

"Just who are you ducking?" Grobie asked, wiping the anxiety of preparing a real meal from her forehead.

"No one. Nothing," he replied as he sat down at the table.

Grobie straightened her Aztec print dress to hug her figure more. "Where did you say your friend was?" she asked again.

Shane Montrose entered perfectly on cue and Grobie blushed a little when she realized he was behind her. He was unshaven and unkempt-looking but still wore a great suit, even though it had obviously been slept in. His eyes were red and yellow and his usual radiating tan was overpowered by a sick gray tone. This was not the same Sugarstick who packed out venues across the country. Shane Montrose looked like a man who tried to keep up his appearance but could no longer afford it. Grobie, however, didn't give a fuck. He was still Shane Montrose.

"Thank you for your hospitality, Mrs. . . . ." Shane said as he entered the kitchen.

"Call me Grobie," Grobie said with a dirty smile. "All the wrestlers call me Grobie."

Curt saw how hard she was putting herself out there and shook his head in disgust. He had liked her at the beginning because she was so overt. Now it sickened him. Simply put, Grobie was a Ring Rat who liked to fuck wrestlers. She was infamous for it up and down the business. Shane Montrose was kind of like her missing card to complete the set.

"Where would you like me?" Shane asked, shamelessly flirting with practiced ease.

She replied, "A couple of inches up in my . . ."

"No!" Curt shouted as he pounded his fist on the table. "I'm sitting right here."

Shane and Grobie silently conceded that Curt had a point. So did the baby, who began to cry in the living area.

Grobie pulled herself back to civility. "There's salt on the table," she advised her guest.

"Thank you," Shane said as he took a seat.

"You going to see to the baby?" Curt asked Grobie.

"He'll be fine in a minute," she replied.

Shane's mere presence was enough to sicken Curt. He didn't want Sugarstick anywhere near his secret family. Or near business, now. He knew Shane was only there because he heard that Danno was calling. It was damn near impossible to keep anything quiet in the wrestling business.

Curt's business was on the verge of collapse. And now he had the extra dead weight of a 50/50 partner around his neck, who wasn't worth a fraction of his initial investment.

Grobie placed her broken, dubious chicken dish in the middle of the table and stood back to judge its perfection. She pushed some peas atop the mound of pinkish meat and hard vegetation and seemed finally pleased. Both men awaited her go-ahead.

"Now, dig in. To the meal I mean," she said to Shane with a dirty wink.

Curt, well trained around Grobie's cooking, avoided the meat altogether, but he happily watched Shane tear into the undercooked bird.

"So how long are you in town?" she asked her guest.

Curt checked his watch and hopped up nervously from his sitting position. "I . . . have to make a call," he said, knocking over his drink.

"Jesus, Curtis," Grobie replied. "Do you have to be a fat fucking elephant?"

Curt took his crying child from the living room and plonked him between Grobie and Shane. "You two continue on. I'll just be a minute," he said.

"Business?" Shane asked.

"Not really," Curt replied. "Personal stuff."

Curt hurried back to the living area, picked up the phone, and dialed. "Hello?" he said, half whispering.

"Is this Curt?" Danno asked.

Curt could hardly contain the relief in his voice. "Danno?"

Danno spoke from his office in New York. "I got your message."

"Do we have a deal?" Curt asked quickly as he walked the long phone cord as far away from the kitchen as he could.

Danno was surprised at Curt's forwardness but, after struggling with his dying business for over a year, Curt was in no position to be coy.

Danno replied, "Yeah, we got a deal. But this is between us. If I hear for a second that the word is out to the other bosses on this deal, then I pull my offer and spend my time blacklisting you. Understand?"

Curt wondered whether Danno meant he would blacklist him *even more*. "I just want out. Going out of business is an expensive thing," Curt said, looking directly at Shane Montrose in Grobie's kitchen.

"I'll buy your territory, Curt," Danno said directly.

Curt held the phone into his palm so Danno couldn't hear him. "Thank you, Jesus," he whispered to himself before reengaging in the conversation.

"Okay," Danno continued. "Give me your number. I have to run some things past Troy and make sure this can all be squared in Lawyerland."

"This line isn't great," Curt lied. "I got a pay phone down the street. I can ring you back." Curt didn't want anyone knowing about his bit on the side or his bastard son.

In the kitchen, Shane watched Curt closely. He didn't buy for a second that the call was personal. Grobie pushed Shane's plate closer to him.

"Eat up," she said. "A body like that can't run on empty."

Shane rose quietly from the table and walked toward Curt.

"You don't mind if I watch you leave?" Grobie laughed.

Shane didn't answer. He was too busy trying to figure out if he was getting cut out of a deal. Too busy trying to calculate whether yet another promoter was trying to fuck him over. He needed his cut now more than at any other time in his life.

Curt heard Shane's footsteps, so he hung up and steadied himself before turning around.

"Do we have wine?" Curt asked Grobie, already knowing the answer. "I won't be long." Curt grabbed his jacket and keys and left.

Ten minutes later Shane was fucking Grobie on the bathroom floor. Like most Rats Shane had had sex with over the years, Grobie didn't seem to be into it. It was like she was somewhere else. It was only when he'd stop and try and catch her eye that she'd snap to and moan a little.

The bathroom door was slightly open. At first Shane was worried about Curt coming back and seeing them. Now he was worried that Curt would come back and *not* see them. So Shane Montrose scuttled back just far enough to poke the bathroom door open further. He was sick of promoters looking at him as dim-witted. They saw the wrestlers as dullards—a necessary evil in the attraction business. There was no way Curt was going to give him a straight story or tell him who was on the call. Shane knew it was Danno. It had to be. But if Curt wouldn't talk to him and Danno wouldn't talk to him, maybe another Garland would.

May 14, 1972
Five months before Annie's murder.
New Jersey.

Shane lay naked beside Annie Garland. The dismal room was small and sweaty, far from what they were both used to. Shane usually liked to pay for a higher-class joint, but he was now counting coins and actively avoiding people who were looking for their money back. Things with Curt were bad. And he smelled a rat.

They both lay without saying a word and Annie wasn't even all that sure that she liked the man beside her. She wanted to blame him, and only him, for making her do these things—these backhanded things that made her sick to her stomach. But in truth, she knew that Shane hadn't done anything more than make the call. She answered him, entertained his requests to meet, and followed him. It was her—and her alone—she hated. But she had a way of making most of that hatred disappear. For a while, anyway.

"I wish you never gave me one of these in the first place," Annie said as she inspected the small pill between her fingers.

Shane grabbed it and threw it into his own smoke-filled mouth.

"He giveth and he taketh away again," he said as he blew a stream of smoke toward a ceiling that had obviously seen a lot of smoke in its day.

Annie rolled onto her side and reached into her purse where plenty more pills were waiting in a small silver box. She thought the box added a little class to a totally classless pursuit. The contents of that little metal tomb held Annie Garland totally and completely.

"Those little things help me do what I do," Shane said of the pills. "They let me go another week and then another year. They let me earn money. They let me walk around."

Annie carefully placed one in her mouth, all ladylike, and swallowed it down with a waiting drink of water. "Me too," she said.

"I got two bum knees, a ripped-up shoulder, and the pain in my back sometimes makes me think of killing myself. What have you got, lady?"

"There's different kinds of pain," she answered simply.

Shane stubbed out his cigarette and turned to her, resting his head in the palm of his hand. "What pain does a woman like you have?" he asked disbelievingly.

Annie could feel the warm, familiar comfort wash over her. It started around her shoulders and worked its way up along the back of her head. "None," she answered. "I've got nothing to worry about."

Shane looked her up and down, taking in every inch of her—something her husband would never do. To Annie, Shane was rougher, more base, more simple than Danno. Over the years it sickened her that she was attracted to Shane Montrose. She beat herself up over the fact that he was two steps away from being an animal. No tact, no manners, no plans, no strategy. Just all instinct, grabbing, and aggression. But he looked at her and wanted her like her husband never would or did. Sometimes she imagined herself being with Shane full time. She knew she wouldn't have to worry about him and his supper; how his clothes looked and what his mood was. She wouldn't have to rear him and prop him up and make sure she placed his keys in the very same fucking place every single morning of their marriage because if they were two inches from that place she would have to come down the stairs and place them in his fat fucking hand.

She was lying beside a man who could, and did, look after himself. She knew Shane was the type of man who lied and fucked dubious women and paid more attention to what he looked like than what his woman looked like. He was attracted to shiny things and dangerous things and things that could harm him. And she thought she loved that. She just wasn't sure. What she did know was that she was tired of fighting it. Tired of wondering. Tired of trying to remember what it was like to be with a man who wanted her. Who at least acted like he loved her. A man with some fight in him. A man who wasn't ready to coast to the end. She was now older and softer in places. But she wasn't ready to be locked in a big house and put on pause until Danno came home.

"What are you thinking about?" he asked as he rubbed his hand around her ribcage and under her breast.

"I'm thinking about my husband," she said as she swallowed another pill.

"Maybe you should take it easy on those."

Annie lay back and waited to forget. Or to not care. Hopefully both, but more than likely the latter.

"Word is he's doing something with Curt?" Shane asked, hoping to sound more chatty than snoopy.

"Who?" she replied.

"Danno."

Annie grabbed Shane's hand and threw it from her body. "Do you think I want you talking about my husband while you feel me up?"

"You brought him up," he said.

Annie wanted to get up and get dressed. Then she didn't want to do anything.

"He'd have me killed if he knew, wouldn't he?" Shane asked in a more somber voice.

Annie smiled. "Danno doesn't have it in him to kill anyone."

"I wouldn't be so sure," he said.

"I can't think of a single thing on this planet that would drive him so nuts he'd do something like that."

"Not even this?"

"Especially not this."

There was a slight pause where they both imagined the outcome of their affair going public.

"I don't want to talk about Danno here," Annie said.

Shane could see his door closing, his opportunity to find out more fading. He needed to know if Curt was telling the truth when he said that Danno wasn't doing a deal. For Shane Montrose, Curt selling to Danno meant there was enough money for Shane to finally get out of his own money troubles.

"He doesn't tell me anything," Annie said, now more relaxed.

"He's never said anything about Curt Magee or Texas?" Shane asked.

"What? I don't know," she answered as she began to melt more into herself.

Shane didn't believe her. He didn't believe her at all. He started to get the gnawing feeling that everyone was about to make a lot of money. Except him. And not making money was an unacceptable situation for Shane Montrose. He had spent a lot of money, and got a loan of even more money, on the promise of his slice coming through the Texas territory. And Shane Montrose knew *his* bankers weren't the suit-wearing kind.

October 11, 1972.
Five days after Annie's murder.
New York.

Shane took in the grounds and the stables but he didn't notice any cars in the drive. Danno's house was huge and square and it stood still and quiet. As the taxi waited, Shane wasn't sure if his being there was such a good idea. Maybe Danno wasn't here? Maybe there were fifty cars parked around the back. Who knew?

He paid the waiting driver from a slab of folded notes. He tipped him a fifty and signed his autograph on a copy of the daily paper.

The headline read: SENATOR TENENBAUM HOME AND RESTING

"Thank you. I saw you wrestle in the Garden many times over the years," the cab driver excitedly told his famous passenger.

Shane nodded politely and stood small under the shadow of the house. He walked cautiously toward the steps as his ride pulled off down the driveway. His breath was stale from drink, but that wasn't anything unusual. His face was rough and his clothes were the same as the day before. He had survived Danno and the wake. Literally. Now he wanted to find out where Curt Magee was hiding. With the bounty Danno had out, Shane knew it was only a matter of time before Danno found out first.

Shane took the first step toward the house. The air smelled different after the rain in this part of New York. It was fresh and

subtle. He took another step while looking around. Danno swung
open his front door and marched toward his visitor. "What the fuck
do you want with me?"

"I . . ." Shane struggled to piece together a sentence that would
make sense.

Danno raised a 12-gauge shotgun and jammed it against the forehead of the petrified man in front of him.

"Danno, please," Shane begged. "Let me . . ."

"What?"

"Let me . . ."

"Let you what?" Danno said as he screwed the barrel of his gun
deeper into the flesh on Shane's head.

"I just . . ."

"You just what? Speak. You fucking tell me why you're at my
door. Tell me why I shouldn't blow your fucking head off on these
steps."

As both men looked at each other, Danno could see it. He didn't
want to acknowledge it, but he could see it. Shane Montrose was lost
too.

"I'm sorry," Shane said simply.

"You keep saying that. What do you want me to say to you?" Danno
tried to raise the same anger that he had a second or two before, but
he couldn't. He whipped the gun barrel away from Shane's head.

"Don't make me kill you," Danno warned as he turned back
toward his house. He was trembling from adrenaline. This wasn't
him. A month ago he would have run from conflict. He was getting
too old to be suspicious of everyone. It was wearing him down. He
wanted to tear the weight out from his stomach—that deadness that
lay in there and twisted back and forth.

"Danno?"

Danno stopped.

"I want to help you," Shane said. "You don't need to get involved
in this. I'd happily . . . tell me where Curt Magee is . . ."

Danno turned and looked Shane dead in the eye, walked back, grabbed him by the jaw bone, and discharged a shot downward, clipping Shane's foot. The pain and shock took a split second to register—but when it did, Shane collapsed, screaming in agony.

"You shot me. You fucking shot me," he roared in disbelief.

"For years I watched her leaving this house and I knew where she was going. The next time I see you," Danno calmly said as he pointed his gun at Shane's head, "I won't aim any lower than your face."

Shane covered up. Danno stood over him long enough to punctuate his dominance. He looked down and saw the broken flesh exposed through the disintegrated designer shoe.

"Now get the fuck out of here," Danno warned as he went back inside and slammed the door.

Danno already knew where Curt was. He didn't need anyone else's help to find him anymore. But he thought he needed someone else's help in killing him.

CHAPTER TEN

Madison Square Garden was the mecca, the spiritual home of the Garlands' wrestling company. Danno's father had run there for years before Danno took over and did the same. Every month they would finish their traveling loop in the sold-out Garden. Every month except this one. Tickets for this one were slow, to say the least.

Ricky walked through the hushed backstage entrance on the ground floor. His shoes tapped along the concrete floor past the rubbish stacked high against the cold brick walls. Above his head a confusion of exposed cables and pipes ran in all directions. The crew had been in all day setting up and getting ready. There were wrestlers from all over the country above his head. And a whole lot of problems, too. Ricky followed the corridor and saw a couple of forklift trucks covered with arena hands taking a smoke break. He nodded in their direction and walked up the ramp, tapping his hand off the battered railing. He took a sharp right and passed a train of pallets, still packed and waiting to be opened. The snugly wrapped silver piping followed him along the ceiling, and large hanging lights lit the way. It was more like a boiler room than the most famous arena in the world.

Another right turn brought him into the jaws of the large service elevator with the worn floor. In it, Ricky felt small and insignificant. He knew that his time in that elevator was probably going to be the only quiet time of the next few days. He pushed the button and the protective cage slid down across the opening. Two metal doors then engulfed the cage like a metal mouth closing, and the floor began to shudder under his feet. The short journey to the backstage area began. This was going to be a hard day, with hard decisions to be made.

All without Danno.

The elevator came to a stop and the doors slid back into hiding. It was noisier now. The backstage area had the hum of people behind doors, laughter in distant hallways. Ricky steadied himself and walked from the elevator through the same double doors he had passed countless times before. He bypassed all of the open and half-open doors and walked directly down to the opening that led onto the arena floor.

"Ricky?" a voice called from behind.

Ricky stopped dead. It was the only voice that could make him stop. He backtracked and peered around the door. It was who he thought it was: Danno.

"I think I've found him," Danno said.

Danno looked unshaven, unkempt.

"How are you doing?" Ricky asked as he approached.

"I think I have him," Danno replied.

"Curt?" Ricky whispered trying to drag Danno's volume down a few notches.

Danno nodded. He was distant and distracted.

"How?"

"We have to go," Danno said as took off, leading the way. "I have a taxi waiting."

Ricky stayed. "Boss?"

Both men were standing inside Madison Square Garden, it was a few hours to bell time, and only one of them had wrestling or business anywhere near to being on his mind.

"I can't," Ricky said.

Danno stopped and looked at his right hand man with confusion on his face. "I said I found him."

Ricky was a loyal soldier, but wrestling was wrestling and business was business. What Danno wanted him to get involved in was something completely different. Something he decided that he didn't want any hand, act, or part in.

"I'm running out of time," Danno said as he began to walk. "They might have someone talking in there already."

"Who might have someone talking?" Ricky asked.

Danno stopped and took a few steps back toward Ricky. "The cops. I got word that someone has turned and is going to rat us out."

"They're fucking with you."

"Not this guy." Danno began to walk again. "I'll fill you in on the way."

"On the way where?"

Ricky marched after Danno and gently grabbed his swinging arm. "I'm staying here," he said with his head bowed. "Unless you tell me that you don't want me here. But that thing you're leaving to do right now. I understand. But . . ."

"But what?" Danno asked.

"That's not . . . I've got . . ." Ricky pointed down to the opening that led out onto the famous arena floor. "That's what I signed up for. With your father before you. And with you."

"You're not coming?"

Ricky very reluctantly shook his head. "No."

"You sure?"

Ricky nodded. "Yeah."

"Well then, you're a fucking faggot," Danno said as he slapped Ricky across the face.

Ricky immediately filled with anger. The outcome of years of trust and hard work and sacrifice in front of them both and it was down to this—an insult with his hand and an insult with his mouth.

"I'm trying to understand," Ricky said. "I'm trying to imagine what it's like to be in your shoes. But if you ever raise your hand to me again you better have an ambulance waiting and not a taxi. You fucking understand me?"

Danno stood in front of him defiantly.

Ricky continued. "And if you don't stop this path you're on, you're going to pull everything down with you. Your life and my life."

Ricky wanted him to stay. He wanted Danno to honor the business. The thing that was still alive and they could do something about. The thing his father built before him and the thing that was handed to him as a gift. A near hundred-year-old gift.

Danno turned away and walked to his cab. He didn't want to go either. But he had to live up to his promise. Even if it meant changing who he was. If Ricky wasn't willing to help then Danno needed to make contact with a man who would.

The city had already made Shane's white bandages stained and dirty. He dragged himself up the stairs of his shitty hotel. Every step was a cruel and painful heave. There was a lump missing from the side of his foot and he was convinced that several of his toes were broken from the sheer velocity of the gunshot blast. It was hard to tell the full extent of the damage without getting an X-ray—and it was hard to get one of those without going to a hospital and attracting attention to himself. More than any of that, he knew he simply didn't have any more time to waste. He needed to get to Curt. And he needed to do it before Danno.

Shane had made a call to a doctor upstate who was very friendly with professional wrestlers. Every town had such a physician, someone who liked big cash money for a call-out and access to his prescriptions book. But even the dubious doctor warned Shane of the dangers of not going to an emergency room. Sugarstick instead left with a clean wound, a tight dressing, and a pocketful of sedatives, barbiturates, and a little bag of powder completely off the books.

He triple-locked his hotel door from the inside and staggered back onto his noisy spring bed. The pain was excruciating. He thought that in all his years of wrestling, and all the injuries that such a life brings, he had developed a significant pain threshold. Maybe the only thing that had kept him moving was that threshold. But this was testing his limits.

He rattled around in his pocket looking for the pills. For the first time in his adult life he was calculating on how many would *not* get him too stoned. Even in intense pain, Shane had to keep his wits about him.

He threw his arm out and slapped around the bedside locker, looking for his watch. In doing so, it slid like a snake onto the floor. "Fuck. You. Fuck . . ."

It was all too much. He began to sob. The room. His foot. Annie. Guilt. His family. Deals being done with him and without him. Paranoia. New York. Danno. The pain. The excruciating pain.

And then his phone rang. The volume of the bell vibrating beside him startled him. He had waited so long to hear it, it took a second for him to decide that the sound was real.

His phone *was* ringing. He just quickly prayed that the voice on the other end was Curt.

Shane slowly picked up the phone. "Hello?"

"Shane?" a scared-sounding voice asked.

It was Curt.

"You alone?" Curt asked.

"Yeah."

"I . . . I . . . don't know what to do here," Curt said.

"Hey, listen. I've . . . I've been up here in New York. I've been smoothing things over. I can . . ." Shane rolled over a little to get closer to his bedside locker. He moaned in discomfort as he pulled a gun from his drawer and checked the chamber. "Tell me where you are and I'll come meet you," Shane said in his most faux-sympathetic voice. "I think we can figure this out."

Danno was in the back of his taxi. The city was full, dirty, and swollen with the sounds of car horns and construction work. It was raining and gray. A bus pulled into traffic in front of them and chugged out a cloud of black smoke as it struggled along its route. In the backseat with him was a discarded newspaper that read: FBI Finds Nixon Aides Sabotaged Democrats.

The whole country was working each other. Power-grabbing from the top all the way down. Danno wished it was still that simple for him. For a split second he forgot the stomach-churning events of the last few days and remembered a time when his business was all about the pieces on the board. He loved to move them around, look for the openings, and make his move. He wasn't a killer. Or at least, he hadn't been born one. But he knew he would have to be one at least once more before his own judgment happened.

He got out of the cab, overpaid the grateful cab driver, and walked into the park. Around him people scurried for his vacated ride, shielding themselves from the rain with anything they could put above their heads. Jackets, newspapers, umbrellas. Danno didn't notice or care about the weather.

Across the street Nestor Chapman sat in his unmarked car, watching. "Any sign?" asked a voice over his radio system.

Nestor picked up the phone-shaped receiver and placed it to his lips, but didn't answer.

"Do you copy?" the voice asked again.

Nestor again didn't answer. He reluctantly put the receiver down and opened his car door.

Danno walked the pathway and scanned passersby to see if they were his contact.

"Danno," Mickey Jack Crisp said from a park bench.

Danno recognized the frame. The outline of his hair. His long, thick sideburns. Danno immediately knew that he was looking at the man who had buried Proctor after Danno put a bullet in his head. That was exactly who he was looking for.

"Mickey?" Danno asked before approaching.

Mickey nodded. He too seemed totally at ease with the torrential rain hopping off the bench under him.

Danno walked closer. "I want you to help me."

Danno passed Mickey an oversized envelope from his coat with Curt's details and a stack of cash in it. "I just need you to bring him to me. I'll do the rest. I have a chartered plane. It's all in there. Let's go."

"Now?" Mickey asked.

"Yes. Now. You got a problem with that?"

Mickey seemed torn. "I can meet you in a couple of hours. I just have to finish something first."

Danno looked at him suspiciously. "It's now or I go and get someone else."

Mickey's mouth was full of questions but Danno just walked on.

Nestor stood under a tree, out of the rain, watching from a distance.

Mickey drove the beaten-up brown Plymouth through the rain toward the airport. Danno noticed Mickey's shoes were mucky and the floor of the car was the same.

"Rain destroys everything," Mickey said.

Danno wasn't so sure. "What's the smell?" he asked.

Mickey decided to elaborate. "I don't have anywhere to stay up here. I was just supposed to come to town and do . . ." Mickey didn't finish the sentence. "And then I was supposed to head back to Florida . . ."

"Florida?" Danno asked.

Mickey nodded. "Some other things came up so I hung around. Bottom line is I've been living out of this car for a couple of days. Sorry about the smell. I wasn't expecting company."

Danno knew somewhere in the back of his head that Mickey was from Florida. He had just forgotten. He thought about the note that was left under his door: THERE'S A HEATWAVE COMING UP FROM FLORIDA. MAKE SURE AND COVER UP.

He looked back as far as his fat body would let him to see if they were being followed. Mickey could sense his sudden jumpiness.

"You doing okay, man?" he asked.

"Yeah," Danno said as he adjusted the mirrors he could reach, to let him see the angles from behind.

Now Mickey was getting jumpy too. "Is there something happening here that I should be aware of?"

Danno shook his head. Unconvincingly.

"You looking for cops?"

"No."

"'Cause I don't mind being followed by anyone else other than cops."

"Yeah? Why's that?"

"'Cause I've got some outstanding business that I don't want to get into with them. So you need to tell me what's going on here or I'm turning this car the fuck around, Danno," Mickey said.

Danno thought about where to start and what Mickey needed to know. "They're tailing us."

"Who is?"

"The cops," Danno answered.

Mickey immediately looked for an off-ramp.

Danno continued, "When we get to the airport, you drop me off at the terminal and go and park. I have a plane waiting for us." He took back Mickey's envelope and wrote the hangar number on the front of it. He could see Mickey wasn't entirely sold. He said, "You drop me off, park the car, and meet me there. If you get there and I don't, I still want you to go do what we've discussed. Only difference is, I want you to hold him there. Alive. I'll make my way to you when the time is right."

Mickey was about to argue all the legitimate issues that would raise.

"I'll give you an extra hundred grand. And tell Little Terry the same. Hundred each."

"Who's Little Terry?"

"My pilot."

Mickey could hear in Danno's voice that Danno wanted to do the dirty end of Mickey's job for him. Again.

"If we get split up, my house phone number is in the information I gave you," Danno said.

"Deal," Mickey said as he put out his hand. Danno obliged. Mickey's firm response gave him some hope.

"But don't let the cops look through this car," Mickey said.

Danno nodded. Mickey made sure to look Danno in the face so Danno would understand how serious he was. "There's a couple of things in this car that could get us both in some trouble."

October 2, 1972.
One week before Annie's murder.
Texas.

Bert *tat-tat-tat*ed on the window. But there was no answer. He tried again. Shane Montrose owed him money and he wasn't leaving. *Tat-tat-tat*. Nothing. Bert checked his watch and took a couple of steps back to look up at the top windows. He was outside a nice house. Big, but not huge. Certainly owned by wealthy people, though. It was freshly painted and there were colorful flowers in the window boxes outside.

"Hello?" Bert called. "Hello?" He walked around the side of the house and cupped his hands at the ground floor window to look inside. It was quiet inside. No signs of life. The place was well kept and orderly. He could see through to the kitchen. It certainly seemed empty.

But it wasn't.

In the broom closet of her kitchen, Crystal Montrose held her breath. She knew what the person outside her house was looking for. Her husband had warned her, moved her someplace safe. But Crystal didn't want to live her life in hiding. She didn't want to live in her brother's place. She wanted to be home.

So that's where she was. In the broom closet of her kitchen, shaking with fear.

"Mommy?" called a child's voice from the stairs.

Crystal didn't have time to warn her five-year-old daughter to be quiet.

"Mommy," she called. "Is Daddy home?"

The little girl was frightened by the sudden quietness downstairs. She knew her mother was usually singing, watching loud TV, or talking up a storm on the telephone.

"Mommy?" she said as she warily looked into the kitchen.

Crystal couldn't move from panic. She tried to "shh" her daughter but she knew her voice was too low to matter.

"Mommy?"

Crystal could hear her little girl's voice begin to tremble. She prayed that the man outside was gone. The scared little girl walked into the kitchen doorway and saw her mother, with tearstains on her cheeks and her finger to her lips, gesture at her to go back up the stairs.

Too late.

The back door burst open with a terrifying crack as the intruder smashed his way in. The little girl screamed and dashed up the stairs. Crystal tried to follow, but Bert pulled her back by two handfuls of her hair.

"Where is he?" Bert shouted.

"I don't know," Crystal screamed as she tried in vain to fight back.

Bert's face was scarred, some of his teeth missing. Her slaps and kicks were having no effect.

"You tell him that if I don't see him within seven days that I'm going to find you and his little girl and set you both on fire."

Crystal turned away in terror as Bert leaned in closer. "You fucking hear me?" he shouted. "Your scumbag husband is going to get you all killed in the worst way imaginable."

Crystal closed her eyes until she could feel his hot breath move away and hear his footsteps head toward her door.

"He has one week to get me my money," Bert said calmly before he left.

His throat was raw from too much smoking and his hands were shaky from too much coke. Shane Montrose was coming home after two weeks on the road and Texas was a huge, awkward state to travel by car. He'd been to Houston, Fort Worth, Dallas, San Antonio, and Austin. Twice. He would now come off the road for a day or two and then hit some smaller "spot" towns in between the loop of Houston, Fort Worth, Dallas, San Antonio, and Austin. Twice. He had the names of the towns and cities playing around in his head like a continuous record.

He was getting too old to be struggling with a state so big. Most of his colleagues were trying to get to San Francisco. Small trips, great weather, home every night. Shane Montrose was a star, but he was a regional star. The guy with the heavyweight title was the national star. Flown everywhere, driven the rest. Best of hotels, more women than he could handle and the biggest money—by far—at the end of the night.

Being home every night sounded great to him on drives like this, but he knew he'd be bored within a week and would be out partying and chasing tail.

That's the reason he was coming home to wife number three.

About five minutes away from home he saw a man walking in the middle of the road waving his arms. Shane checked the rearview mirror and saw that his was the only car on the road—the dark back road. It looked way too risky, like the start of a setup. Especially in Sugarstick's addled mind. The guy in the road would get Shane to slow down and then someone else would jump him from behind. *Fuck it.* He floored it and headed straight for the wandering man.

The last couple of years had all been about surviving, avoiding lenders, and making it to the next day. Curt was only paying him a percentage of the gate in every town, "until Danno comes to his senses."

The more he picked up speed, the closer he got, the more terrified the man in the road looked.

"Hey," the man in the road shouted.

"Don?" Shane wondered as he skidded to a stop just in time.

Don sat silently in Shane's passenger seat as they pulled into Don's driveway. Don had just filled Shane in on what happened and Shane didn't know what to say.

"You know my sister isn't the type to worry for no reason," Don said as Shane took his keys from the ignition.

"I know."

"Your shit is getting serious now," Don said. "And I love my sister, but I don't want anyone kicking in my door looking for you neither. You hear me?"

"I know," Shane replied.

"So fucking do something about it," Don said as he left the car.

Shane followed. He could see Crystal sitting out on the porch. She was smoking—he'd never seen her do that.

"Where's the little one?" Shane asked as he approached.

Crystal stood and walked into his path. "She's asleep. Finally."

Don entered his house and left them to it.

"I'm going to make this simple, Shane," she said. "I don't know what you do on the road. I can guess, I can imagine, but I don't want to know. But when your actions send a man to our home to do us harm—and he was deadly serious—I don't know what to do anymore."

Shane put out his arms for a hug. "Baby, I'm sorry."

Crystal began to cry. "I couldn't even call the cops because I don't know if you're involved in something illegal or not. I don't know what to do to protect my child."

Shane put his hand at the back of her head and tried to coax her in closer to him. She pushed him away. "You go back out there and fix whatever it is you've dragged us all into. Do you hear me? You moved us again with promises of a mansion and cars and vacations every other month. Where is it? Where's the deal you made? I bet everyone else is making more than you. As usual there's a pot of money somewhere and everyone else is dipping into it except my husband. Mister fucking Big Time. The one the whole business is laughing at. Again. Open your eyes. You're a joke."

Crystal walked into her brother's house and slammed the door.

October 11, 1972.
Five days after Annie's murder.
New York.

Matthew Miller paced along 32 Old Slip. He was late and smoking. He knew the second part of his day was just starting even though he could feel the evening coming on. On the opposite side of the street he could see his building, long and narrow, beside the East River. No one in his department knew yet that the coming Christmas would be their last in that building. He was just waiting on word to see if his First Precinct was, in fact, going to be amalgamated with the Fourth. If that was the case, then his building wouldn't be big enough to hold both crews. They'd certainly have to move. With that move, he hoped he'd be captain over both houses. All he needed was to prove himself with a big "get." And nothing was bigger in the NYPD than getting someone who stabbed a US senator.

"Captain Miller?" called a voice from behind.

Miller stopped and turned. He knew the voice but didn't know from where. He saw a man hurry toward him. He recognized him as the head of the New York State Athletic Commission, the governing body for both boxing and wrestling in New York. Amateur wrestling he could handle, but professional wrestling made him sick.

"Sir," called Melvin. "My name is Melvin Pritchard. I believe we spoke on the phone."

Miller nodded and extended his hand. "Nice to meet you," he said as he continued walking toward his building. The captain wanted someone for the senator's attack, but he felt Melvin was way off in his theory that a bunch of wrestling guys were involved.

"Can I just have a minute . . ." Melvin said as he followed. He had spent a lot of his time trying to get professional wrestling, and Danno Garland, put under the federal spotlight. Up till this point he'd failed in that regard. "I was wondering how your investigation is going? With regard to Senator Tenenbaum?"

"I can't comment," said the captain.

Both men dodged the oncoming crowds.

"And Danno Garland?" Melvin asked.

The captain stopped. "I can't comment on him either. Look, I appreciate the information you gave us over the phone, I really do, but the senator is saying he didn't see anything that can help us."

"Do you know where Danno was the night the senator was attacked?" Melvin asked.

Miller could see the lamps at either side of the precinct door glowing a couple of hundred feet away. He wanted to keep walking, but he was sure he was going to have to hear Melvin talk one way or the other.

"No. I don't know where he was," the captain answered.

"He was with me." Melvin paused. "He called to meet me in JFK that night and the night before. He sat in front of me and said nothing. As a matter of fact, he did nothing for hours. He just watched the clock."

Miller was failing to see how this was implicating Danno in any way.

Melvin continued, "He used me as an alibi. He made me recite the date and the time before he stood up and left. That was the night the senator got attacked."

Miller was unimpressed. "It means nothing. We'll keep looking. I can promise you that." He turned from Melvin and started to stride off.

"Sir," Melvin called.

Miller turned around. He was short on patience. "Sir, indeed," Miller replied. "This fucking city is choking. The Bronx is burning; we don't have the money to pay for our schools. I'm hearing about German Shepherds being posted down in the subway. Right here, where you're standing, we had to bag up three Chinks who welshed on a fucking bet last week." Miller could see he had Melvin's attention. "I don't give a fuck about what you think a bunch of con men are doing to the spirit of competition."

Captain Miller was sure he made his point before he turned to walk away again.

"Did you know his wife was murdered?" Melvin asked. His parting words stopped Miller in his tracks.

"What?" the captain asked.

"I still have to oversee these people as head of the Athletic Commission. I hear things when I'm with them. There's something going on. Danno's wife was killed in Texas a few of days ago," Melvin said.

Miller seemed genuinely taken aback. "She was murdered?"

Melvin nodded. He could see he now had the captain's attention. "We were trying to shut Danno's business down. The senator and I. We were one day away from getting the ball rolling when the senator was attacked. Or he was made an example of, I should say. A week or so later, Danno's wife turns up dead in a hotel in Texas. I don't know how one thing links the other. And maybe they don't. But I thought you should know."

The captain took a second to digest what Melvin was saying.

Melvin continued, "I don't know *what's* happening, but *something* is happening, and they're finally starting to get sloppy."

Captain Miller wanted to know what that *something* was now too. He thanked Melvin and left him standing on the sidewalk.

He was now at least curious as to what was going on. And he was even more curious to find out where Nestor Chapman was.

The backstage area was packed with wrestlers stretching, drinking, pacing, and going through their matches. New faces from all over the country had descended on the Garden. Ricky had the Book in his hand with all the matches listed out.

"Where's Ginny?" Ricky asked someone from the ring crew.

He was pointed toward the arena floor. Ricky should have known. He marched through the short tunnel and could see Ginny in the ring with a couple of other, younger-looking rookies. The further Ricky got along the floor the more he could see a small audience of wrestlers in the stands, watching the ring. Ginny was on all fours and was talking to Oscar Dewsbury, who was standing behind him. The same Oscar that Ricky had grabbed by the throat the day before. What Ginny couldn't see was Oscar pretending to fuck him from behind to pop the wrestlers watching in the stands. Oscar was miming, to the delight of the onlookers, while pretending to slap Ginny in the back of his head.

The other person in the ring was a stranger to Ricky. A stranger who was trying to hold in his laughter at the degrading scene in front of him.

Ginny spoke to the visitor, "So when you get scooped up for a slam you tuck your chin in and make sure that your feet come down to protect your kidneys. The more points that hit the mat the better."

"What's going on?" Ricky asked as he approached the ring and jumped up onto the apron.

Oscar immediately jumped up and dropped his head in feigned respect.

"Who's this?" Ricky wanted to know of the stranger in the ring.

The small audience of wrestlers in the stands left quickly. Ricky parted the ropes and entered the ring.

"That's . . . I forget his name. He's an All-American from the State of Michigan," Ginny said of the visitor. "He wants to get into the business."

"Is that right?" Ricky asked as he approached Oscar in the ring.

"He's my cousin," Oscar answered without looking up. He knew that Ricky had seen what he was doing behind Ginny's back. "He wants to try out . . ."

"And you let him in this ring?" Ricky asked.

"You said it was okay," Ginny intervened.

Ricky knew that Oscar had filled Ginny full of bullshit. "I said it was okay?" Ricky asked Oscar.

Oscar was getting nervous at Ricky's questioning. "No, Mr. . . ."

Ricky stopped him mid-sentence with a short right hand that knocked him out clean.

"Hey, hey," Ginny said as he used the ropes to get himself off the mat.

Ricky put his hand up to keep Ginny at arm's length. He wasn't done yet. He went over to the outsider. The one who had been laughing. The one he'd never even seen before. "You see, the thing you must have in this business is respect," he said. "Respect earns you the right to stand in this ring." Ricky unzipped his jacket and threw it over the top rope. "What's your name?"

"Franklin," the All-American answered. He was stocky with a huge neck and cauliflower ears from years of grappling.

Ricky pulled the young man close to his face. "What we do in this ring is no fucking joke."

The amateur wrestler gripped Ricky's wrists but he couldn't stop Ricky from hoisting him into the air and dropping him hard onto his neck and head, folding him up like an accordion.

Franklin's sporting pride made him stumble to his feet, but he was clearly stunned and in pain.

"Men have broken their backs to be in this ring in this arena," Ricky said as he grabbed Franklin and slid his arm under his chin and began to choke him. "So you don't fucking belong here."

Franklin began to turn a shade of purple and the veins in his eyes began to break from the pressure of the hold. Ginny quietly tried to loosen the hold by putting himself between Ricky and the All-American.

"C'mon. It's only this fake stuff that you hear about. Not like what you do, hah?" Ricky asked the flailing young man in his clench. Ricky released the choke and Franklin flopped to the mat without any control.

Ginny pushed Ricky back into the opposite corner and whispered, "What are you doing, Ricky?"

"They're mocking you," Ricky said as looked over Ginny's shoulder to see what damage he had done.

"I was showing them the basics. That's what they pay me to do," Ginny answered.

"No one pays you," Ricky said.

Ricky dropped to the mat and rolled outside. He grabbed Franklin's arm and dragged him out of the ring and dropped him on the floor.

"Someone get this piece of shit out of this building," Ricky shouted toward the wrestlers in the back.

"And tell him," Ricky said to Ginny about Oscar, "he's fired when he wakes up."

Ricky left the ringside area and was ready for the event that night. Fucking show time.

CHAPTER ELEVEN

Danno walked toward the small, white, sharp-nosed plane that sat in wait on the runway. He felt like he was only hours away from making good on the promise to his wife. Tanner Blackwell, as promised, passed on Curt's whereabouts in exchange for the bounty Danno put out there—and one of the heavyweight titles.

In normal circumstances, Danno would never give Tanner the honor of having a world champion in his territory. But there was nothing normal about this day.

Curt was missing from all his usual spots. No sign of him in his favorite bar, restaurant—even his ex-wife's place. He had disappeared when the word went out that Danno was looking for him. Now Curt was hiding himself away with the girl he didn't want anyone to know about, who had his child he didn't want anyone to know about.

But now Danno knew. And he was coming.

"Sir?" called a uniformed police officer as he and his partner appeared behind Danno on the runway. "Sir," the officer continued. "Mr. Garland?"

Fuck!

Danno kept walking, hoping he'd make it to the plane before the realization of what was happening behind him caught up.

"Danno!" the officer shouted.

Danno knew this was something he couldn't out-run. "What?" Danno said over his shoulder.

In the distance he could see the steps of his plane still connected and waiting for him.

"Turn around, sir."

Danno knew time was running out. He needed to get to Curt Magee before he disappeared again. He should have been more worried about Shane Montrose getting there first.

"*Sir,*" came a much more impatient voice.

Danno conceded and turned away from his plane.

One of the police officers stepped forward. "You have to come with us, sir."

They had nothing concrete, but that wouldn't stop them from impeding his travel with questioning and anything else they could think of to make his life harder. Captain Miller didn't trust Danno to leave and not come back. All he could do was get his men to stall him.

Danno looked back toward his plane as he was escorted away. He saw his plane door closing without him.

Inside the airport, the most flamboyant strut in all of professional wrestling was unrecognizable. Shane Montrose limped and grimaced and dragged his loosely bandaged foot. He held the walls of JFK International as he walked, toe to heel, across its crowded floor. He made it to the American Airlines desk with the same panicked relief as a drowning man who barely made it to land. "Dallas," he said to the perfectly polished woman at the desk. He tried to control the sound of pain leaving his mouth as she studied him a little.

"Are you okay, sir?" the middle-aged woman asked.

Shane slammed a mixed ball of cash onto the counter and nodded. He was trembling and sweaty.

"Sir?" she asked again with a concerned voice. "Is everything all right?"

Shane ignored the question. "Can you just get me a ticket?"

"One moment, please," she said as she rose from her position and looked around the terminal.

Shane pocketed his money and pushed himself away from the counter. "I'll just be a second."

The ticket agent's eyes scoured the room more frantically. "I just want to get you some help, sir."

Shane mumbled about "washing up" and painfully scurried toward the restroom.

Inside, he locked himself in a small vacant cubicle and sat on the toilet seat. His foot was unmercifully throbbing as he lifted it from the wet floor and laid it across his opposite thigh. He rested his clammy forehead against the cubicle wall and openly cried in pain. It was wearing on him and he didn't know how much longer he could avoid the lure of the strong sedatives in his pocket. At this rate he wasn't going to make it onto the flight. He looked too suspicious and he was drawing attention to himself.

Shane removed the gun from his jacket and wrapped it time and again in toilet paper until it was covered completely and its shape was indistinguishable. What was he thinking bringing that into an airport?

He steadied himself and exited the cubicle into the empty restroom. He dropped his gun in the trash can before walking again to the desk where he found the same lady.

"Sir?"

"I'm sorry," Shane said, immediately cutting her off. "It's been a hell of a day."

He read her name tag. "Neve."

The woman stood and looked over the counter at the disheveled man in front of her. He was pasty, gaunt, and sweaty. His clothes were creased and unwashed. He had a giant dirty bandage around his foot, and he struggled to stand.

"That's a nice name. Neve," he said.

She was unimpressed.

"I have to get to Texas, ma'am."

"And why is that?"

"You want the truth?"

"Yes, sir, I do."

Shane gingerly took a step forward. "Because I just left my nephew in county morgue about an hour ago. And now I have to go and tell my brother that his son is dead." Shane pressed down on his own injured foot, which quickly brought tears to his eyes. "The little boy was with me. And we crashed. And all I got was this," he said nodding to his foot. "And he . . ." Shane could see the counter lady beginning to melt. "And I have to tell my brother face to face. I have to do that. Even if it means going like this. Now can you help me?"

"Hello?" Lenny half-heartedly shouted around the side of Mrs. Dumont's house. Even though he had grown up next door, Lenny hadn't been on her property since he was a child. And with good reason. He could never really look her in the eye since the time she whupped him right outside her house because his left ball was hanging out as he ran up and down outside her house. Lenny had made his pals laugh. Mrs. Dumont had made Lenny cry shortly thereafter.

"Mrs. Dumont?" he said again, gently, at the side of her house.

Lenny had no choice but to talk to her. She had the key to his parents' house next door.

Lenny opened the front door and Luke charged inside like a crazy midget. James Henry waddled in behind him before falling over. Lenny stepped over his downed child and walked directly to the fridge. Inside, his mom had left him home-cooked food, just like she promised she would. It was labelled and perfectly stacked.

"OK guys, let's go and get you settled in," Lenny said.

It wouldn't take long as Lenny hadn't packed much, and he had concentrated most of his suitcase on diapers.

Luke ran upstairs and Lenny walked through the kitchen to the little door in the pantry. He opened it and stepped directly into his father's small garage. Lenny flipped the switch and there she was—his father's black and silver Ambassador convertible—locked up tightly, with less than a foot of room around each side. It looked as big as a tank in Mr. Long's tiny garage, but the car was only a two-seater. Lenny's father loved it so much that he ended up never touching it, driving it, or letting anyone else go near it. The keys were normally in the ignition, but not with Lenny coming to visit. His father didn't trust him for one second not to take the car out for a drive. Didn't matter. Lenny ran his hand underneath the work bench in the corner until he felt the keys, hidden in his father's "secret" place.

Lenny would take the car into the city. He couldn't resist it any longer. He had to get back in front of the matches, and today there was wrestling at the Garden.

"Who wants to go and see some wrestling?" Lenny shouted.

There was no reply. The walls were thick in his parents' old house so Lenny stepped from the garage back into the kitchen and shouted, "Who wants to go and see some matches in Madison Square Garden?"

Upstairs, Luke could hear his father but he didn't reply and hoped he wouldn't ask again.

"I said, who wants to go and see some wrestling matches?"

Mickey Jack Crisp felt at odds with his surroundings. He was standing at the back of a cruising Gulf Stream II, making himself a cocktail. His life was a bit like that since he started getting work from these wrestling guys. He noticed the bosses who didn't have power were running matches at high schools and bars while the one who called all the shots got champagne arrivals on private jets. There was no in-between in the wrestling business: you were either a star or you were a nobody. You were either on top or you were simply treading water. Not that Mickey was complaining. The stack of cash he had been paid to do this job was so thick that it was uncomfortable in his jeans—even when split up and stuffed into his pockets.

And he didn't even have to kill the guy. The old boss man said he was going to handle that, just like he did with Proctor King. Mickey had been sorry to see Proctor, the man who brought him into this business, get his head blown off like that. But Mickey, like a stray dog, was willing to go with whoever grabbed his leash and treated him well. Cruising thousands of feet above Tennessee, sucking on a fresh strawberry, would tick the "treated well" box, and at the moment, Danno Garland held the leash.

Shane sat in first class beside a very uncomfortable old lady who didn't like the look of the man beside her. He was perspiring profusely, moaning in pain, and his once-white bandages were struggling to keep the dirt out and the blood in.

Shane rolled his head toward the small rounded window and counted down the minutes till he landed in Dallas. Annie was all he could think about. He would land and make this horrible situation go away.

CHAPTER TWELVE

Danno sat handcuffed in the back of the police car. The arresting officers had both entered a gas station about a mile outside the airport and failed to come back. Danno struggled, but he couldn't reach the door to let himself out. Ten minutes or more passed before Danno saw Nestor approaching the patrol car. Nestor opened Danno's door, pulled him out, and escorted him away.

"Say nothing and come with me," Nestor said as he un-cuffed Danno and led him by his forearm to another, unmarked car.

Danno wasn't sure, but he wasn't fighting either. The car he was going to seemed like a better deal than the car he had just left.

"You're my prisoner now," Nestor informed Danno as he opened his passenger side door.

Danno guardedly got in and watched Nestor come around and get in the driver's side.

"How about I drop you home?" Nestor asked.

"How about you tell me what the fuck it is you want from me?" Danno replied.

Nestor started his car. "Why don't we do mine first?"

Nestor backed out of the parking lot and saluted the two officers in his rearview as they appeared, perfectly timed, like this kind of thing happened all the time.

"You starting to see that I'm on your side yet?" Nestor asked.

"Of course you are," Danno replied sarcastically.

Nestor laughed a little and tapped his cigarette pack off the dashboard. He offered Danno a smoke, which Danno refused. Nestor picked himself one from the pack with his lips.

"You really haven't had to think that much about my side of the fence before, have you Danno?" Nestor said. "You guys have been great in keeping the cops away from you for a long, long time."

Nestor considerately rolled down his window and waved his smoke outside. "I'm like a subcontractor," Nestor proudly said. "Your guy gives me a little something to make sure you stay out of trouble."

Danno didn't answer. He was an expert at saying nothing when necessary.

"Troy. Troy Bartlett," Nestor said. "He's the guy who's going to rat you out."

That got Danno interested. He hadn't seen or heard from his lawyer in days. If the cops did have someone who was willing to roll him, Troy Bartlett wouldn't be a shock. He was a dirty lawyer with few or no morals. That's exactly what you needed when you were starting an empire, but it was the last thing you needed when you were controlling one.

Nestor waited to see if Troy's name knocked Danno's tongue loose. "Hey, listen," Nestor said, starting to lose his cool a little. "I fucking put my ass on the line back there, so you better stop treating me like some junkie dirtbag or something. You hear me?"

Danno still wasn't talking. Nestor flicked his half-smoked cigarette out the window and reached around inside his jacket pocket.

"Here," he said as he handed Danno an envelope. "This is for you. Thought you might appreciate getting these back a little earlier." Nestor dropped the envelope in Danno's lap. "It's your wife's things. What they found on her when . . . I got them for you."

Even Danno couldn't hide the pain of holding her things. His eyes welled up.

"It's true, man. I'm on your side," Nestor said. "I got a friend of mine to do me a favor and get me that. I'm trying to fucking show you."

Danno immediately composed himself, wiped his eyes, and pocketed his wife's things. But he didn't speak or even look at Nestor.

"Fuck this." Nestor slammed on the brakes and leaned across Danno to open his door. "Out," Nestor said. "When you open that envelope and see I'm not bullshitting you, you give me a call. And make it soon."

Danno got out on the side of the highway before Nestor skidded off without him. Danno took the envelope from his pocket but couldn't bring himself to open it. Not there. Not on the side of road. And not until he finished his job.

As Danno walked to find a phone, he wondered again where Lenny Long had disappeared to.

Backstage at the Garden, Ricky sat with the Book on his lap. It was full of match ideas, possible outcomes, and future matchups. The page in front of him was now full of brackets and tournament conclusions. Ideas written and scribbled out; names circled; lines drawn and redrawn. Ricky, Tanner, and Joe sat in a small room off the main corridor and agreed on the match outcomes, one painful agreement after the other. All while the audience in the arena got to see their decision play out in almost real time.

"What are we up to?" Tanner asked.

"The semi-finals," Ricky answered, looking at his watch. "And that match is starting in under ten minutes. We need to agree on a finish here so I can get that decision to the Boys."

It had been a slow few hours with negotiation after negotiation. Everyone wanted their guys to look good, but someone had to lose.

"I want my guy up against a sneaky Jap," Tanner said.

Joe and Ricky looked at each other to clarify if they'd both heard the same thing.

"A Jap?" Joe asked. "There's no Japanese wrestlers here."

"Then fucking find one. I want to position my guy as a real patriot. A fucking American hero," Tanner answered. He was working on his own plan in his own Book. And Tanner's Book was still trading off old prejudices from the forties. He continued, "We have an African, a Chink, a Samoan, a German, three Americans, and a Limey. So we need to tell the Samoan guy that he's now a Jap. Same fucking eyes. Nobody knows the difference."

Ricky was done arguing. He just shrugged in Joe's direction.

"Can you do that, Ricky?" Joe asked.

Before Ricky could answer, Tanner was mouthing off again. "He's going to have to get a loan of some karate . . . eh . . . tights or something," Tanner said without looking up from his doodling. "And I don't like the finish of the main event either."

Ricky wasn't having that. "You don't like what, Tanner?"

In one sentence the tone of the room completely changed.

"My guy should go over," Tanner replied. "On his own. One champion."

"That wasn't the deal," Ricky said.

Tanner kept scribbling his own notes. "Yeah, well, I'm thinking about changing the deal. Two champions doesn't sound like that great of a scenario to me no more."

Ricky had enough but he knew he wasn't a boss and couldn't force anything in this scenario. "Joe?"

Joe stood up, "We voted, Tanner. Your guy *and* Ricky's guy both get the pin and a title each. That's what we decided."

Tanner rubbed out his last scenario and blew the eraser residue from his page. "I'm not feeling that anymore."

Ricky looked at his watch. They were out of time and he was out of patience. If he as booker or Joe as chairman couldn't get Tanner to see sense, Ricky knew someone who would. "You want to go and tell the giant you're changing his match?" Ricky asked.

Tanner took a second before realizing that there was no way he could just go into business for himself and beat the giant. Two champions it was. "Yeah, well, make sure I get my fucking Jap."

Lenny Long knew his way around Madison Square Garden. He knew all the hallways, the seating layout, and the people who worked there. But taking a baby in there might be pushing it a bit.

"Helen, please," he said through the will-call window. "I just want to watch a couple of matches and then I'll come straight back for him."

The woman in the ticket booth was shaking her head adamantly. "No way, Lenny. I'm working here."

Luke was holding his father's hand tightly. He didn't want to go anywhere without his father. James Henry was asleep in Lenny's arms despite the noise.

"I've just gotten off a flight and I haven't seen the Boys in days. I just want to . . ."

Lenny could see that Helen wasn't going to budge. He'd just have to watch his own children. "Fuck it," he mumbled to himself.

Lenny dragged his older son by the arm and guarded the baby as he passed through the rowdy fans. He was bare-chested under his coat because he had taken off his shirt and tied it around his baby's head to stifle the noise.

"What do you think of this, son?" Lenny stooped and asked Luke. The boy couldn't yet see anything above the darkness of the huddled crowd. Lenny didn't wait for a reply as he marched them to section 422, row B, seat 4. He'd only paid for one seat so they'd just have to share.

The closer they got to their spot, the more the crowd thinned out. A lot. Lenny was taken aback by how small the audience was in the mezzanine level. The ringside was tight and looked good, but the farther he ran his gaze up along the nosebleeds, the worse it looked.

"How long are we going to be here?" Luke asked with his hands on his ears.

Even with the small crowd, chants and cheers rattled around the Garden like noisy, aggressive old ghosts. They had just made it in time for the main event. Lenny opened his program, like someone starving might look at a menu. It had only been days since he was last around this world, but to Lenny it was days too long. He truly had no idea about how much had changed since he left Florida to start his new life away from wrestling.

The curtain was flung open and out came the giant frame of the man Lenny now knew as Chrissy. To this audience he was the most despised man in all of wrestling—undefeated for years and likely to be so for years to come. But more recently, and much more importantly to the New York crowd, he was the one who no-showed the biggest main event of all time. After years of buildup and bad feeling. A stadium packed to the rafters. Babu simply didn't show up to Shea Stadium. They didn't know his no-show had zero to do with him. And the rules of wrestling meant they never would.

The Garden's small house was a "fuck you" to the company he wrestled for. As if the point hadn't been made enough, they also threw cups of liquid and trash at Babu as he ambled up the wooden steps and through the ropes.

"Go fuck yourself, you coward," roared someone from behind Lenny.

"Champ?" Lenny shouted, even though he knew there was no way Babu could hear him. "Champ?"

"Ring the bell before he chickens out of the match, ref," shouted another voice.

It was always good for the heel to rile the crowd. That's what they were there for. That was their job. And they would do almost anything to get that heat from the stands. But Babu was now the owner of "bad heat." That was the reaction that no wrestler wanted. People would pay for "good heat." The kind where you would pay to see someone get their ass kicked. That was "good heat." "Bad heat" was the other kind. The kind where a crowd just didn't want to see you or walked to the concession stand when you came through the curtain. Or worse—stayed home. "Bad heat" got a low-card wrestler fired, a mid-card wrestler sent to another territory, and a champion wrestler stripped of the belt.

"Ladies and gentlemen," said the ring announcer into the hanging mic. "This is a semifinal match to ultimately determine the NWC Heavyweight Champion of the World, and is one fall to a finish. Introducing to you now, first, the challenger, from Orange County, Florida, weighing in at two hundred and eighty-four pounds, Flawless Franco."

The crowd clapped respectfully. Franco was up from Florida and no one in the Garden knew who he was.

The ring announcer with the pot belly and slicked-back hair continued. "And in the other corner, coming to you from deepest, darkest South Africa, weighing in at four hundred and fifty pounds, the former heavyweight champion of the world . . . BABUUUUUUU."

The crowd lost it. The ones who did pay to see him just wanted to let him know how much they fucking hated him.

The bell at ringside sounded over and over to try to start the match. But Lenny knew that Chrissy, the man everyone else knew as Babu, wasn't happy. Lenny's own shouting toward the ring had his baby boy in floods of tears. His tiny mind couldn't seem to process why it was so dark and so angry.

Lenny never even noticed.

"Dad?" Luke said.

Lenny continued to chant and whoop as the bell rang.

"Dad?" Luke repeated and pulled on his father's sleeve.

Lenny looked down to see his elder son's face.

"Look," Luke said, pointing at his little brother.

Lenny saw James Henry was in distress. He was tired and his face was red and warm. Lenny desperately wanted to stay. He wanted to find out what was happening and why the Garden was so empty. He wanted to see Danno and Ricky.

He wanted back in.

Babu turned his back on cue so Franco could hit him from behind. The giant stumbled slightly toward the corner of the ring with the impact from the devious blow. Franco charged him with his shoulder and threw a cluster of punches to Babu's huge body.

"Choke me," Babu whispered to his opponent.

Flawless Franco duly obliged.

"Low blow," Babu said as he again turned his back.

The referee played his role now too by rushing around to ask Babu if he could continue, while cleverly turning his own back on Franco in the process. Flawless, being the bad guy, waited for the ref to look away before dropping to one knee and uppercutting Babu right in the nuts. That one brought the giant to one knee. The crowd couldn't believe Babu was getting so roughed up so early in the match. Franco took advantage of his stunned opponent by biting the top of Babu's skull and ripping at his eyes. The referee saw it this time and intervened, only to have Franco sidestep him and rush Babu again. Elbow to the head, knee to the body. The giant was in serious trouble, rocking and reeling from the ferocity of the attack. Franco again expertly put his frame between Babu and the referee before driving his thumb into the neck of his huge adversary. Babu barely held onto the ropes and grabbed his throat like it was near impossible for him to even breathe. The audience rose to their feet. They knew they were seeing something unusual here. Babu didn't get manhandled like this. It just didn't happen.

Franco saw his opportunity to pounce on his downed prey as he ran to the turnbuckle while the audience booed his cheating. Both Franco and Babu knew exactly what they had to do to get the New York crowd back behind the giant. Franco needed to use every cheap shot and low blow in the book, and Babu needed to sell those moves more than any giant should. It was hard to feel sorry for a seven-foot man in a fight with someone who was considerably smaller—unless the smaller man was a cheating, cocky asshole who was getting away with breaking all the rules.

"I'm going to be the next champion, and there's nothing any of you can do about it," Franco shouted out into the crowd, and they played their part and rained down on him with jeers and insults. He climbed slowly and dramatically to the second turnbuckle as the noise in the Garden rose considerably. Franco snarled at the crowd and turned himself toward Babu in the ring. The giant was down and having a hard time breathing. The ref was concerned about letting him even continue. Franco deliberately rolled down his knee pad and patted his "exposed" knee cap like it was the secret weapon to killing off a giant. He raised his hands and bathed in the chorus of boos before launching himself into the air and landing, knee first, onto the throat of Babu.

"That was the chest, ref. The chest." Franco shouted far more loudly than he needed to. "That was a clean strike."

The whole building disagreed and the ref took a second to think about his call.

"Disqualify him. Ring the bell," came the shouts from the darkness of the seats.

But before the referee could decide anything, Babu rose like an incensed demon from the deep and stood ominously in wait for Franco to turn around. The building screeched its approval as the giant stood in wait with his fists clenched and a look of rage on his face. Franco turned perfectly into a huge boot to the face, which he sold by flopping into ropes like he had just been hit with a truck. Babu miraculously shook off his throat issues and shot Franco around like a rag doll: Into the turnbuckle, hip toss into the center of the ring, up for slam. The giant was on a roll and he could hear the people come with him. With one hand he peeled Franco from the mat and lifted him into a bear hug. Franco kicked and struggled like he was actually being squeezed to death by a bear. The ref was right there with his hand in the air, ready to step in if the move got too dangerous. Within seconds Franco was limp and being swung from side to side with ease as the referee finally called for the bell.

"Now," the referee shouted. "Ring the bell. The giant is going to kill him."

As Franco lay prone on his shoulder, Babu whispered "thank you" to his opponent. Babu was on his way to a world title.

Lenny walked from the Garden with his little boys both quietly sucking on stacked popsicles. He was feeling slightly put upon, but not enough to be angry or anything. Fact was, after years on the road and having no responsibilities as a father, things had changed. He wasn't any good at being a parent yet, but he wanted to be. He wanted to be a wise father, someone they both sought out when life began to settle into its normal patterns. He even felt a little good about leaving the match. He felt like a grown-up. A grown-up trying to do the right thing by his family.

As he carried one son and let the other swing from his arm, Lenny felt like his father must have felt before him. He felt like a man. A proper, solid, doing-what-he-should man.

For once in his life, toughness had nothing to do with it.

CHAPTER THIRTEEN

October 11, 1972.
Five days after Annie's murder.
Texas.

Shane couldn't break through the thick hedges at the back of Curt's house. They were just too dense, and he was just too injured, to try to bore his way through them. He was tired and tortured but determined to surprise the man who signed him, wooed him, ignored him, conned him, and threatened him. He needed to get into Grobie's house to get at Curt before Danno arrived.

And he knew that couldn't be far from happening.

He grabbed two hopeful fists of green and hoisted himself toward the top of the large hedges, like a drunken child trying to climb atop a camel. Shane's awkward, one-legged attempt to scale the hedges only served to wake the neighborhood dogs with the noise of branches snapping and the leaves rustling under his weight. As the dogs barked he threw himself over the hedge and fell into the yard. The paved portion of the yard. He lay stunned, in pain, and tried desperately to refill his totally emptied lungs. He wasn't sure exactly which part of him was the sorest, but at least he was in.

October 8, 1972.
One day before Annie's murder.
Texas.

Curt Magee and Shane Montrose sat opposite each other in a shitty steakhouse about a hundred miles outside of Austin. It was small and smoky and the sauces sat hardened at the top of their glass bottles. Shane sat with his head dropped. Not in all his years as a wrestling star had the Sugarstick hoped to *not* be noticed. But it was amazing how a huge loan from a serious money lender could turn an extrovert inward.

"I have to wear a fucking leisure suit, Curt," Shane mumbled under his breath. "Do you know what it's like for me to have to wear this shit?"

The waitress slipped a dry steak supper under each of their noses and then smiled at Shane before she left.

"Where's my fucking money?" Shane demanded.

"What money?"

"I swear to God that if you try and tell me that you're not selling the territory to Danno fucking Garland, I will stab you in the throat right here."

There was no point in lying. Curt knew it. "Tomorrow."

"Tomorrow?" Shane asked, a little surprised at Curt's abrupt honesty.

"Yeah. Tomorrow."

"What time?"

"Eight. I'll pick you up," Curt said.

Shane struggled for words. "Ah . . . just like that?"

"Like what?"

"Just like that we have a deal? You're telling me now in this shitty fucking place?"

"How do you think I feel? Huh?" Curt said. "I'm fucking losing everything here. I have Danno, the fat prick, buying me out of business just so I can pay your fucking contract."

"How much? And he's buying *us* out of business," Shane replied.

"Forty grand," Curt lied.

"Forty thousand dollars?" Shane said. "Each?"

Curt shook his head.

Shane couldn't believe what he was hearing. "Forty grand?"

Curt motioned for Shane to keep his voice down. "I don't have TV. Haven't in a long time. Our tickets numbers are in the toilet; I don't have any talent. Except you, of course. He's buying the right to operate here. That's all. He's buying my territory with nothing in it."

"*Our* fucking territory."

Curt shook his head, mumbled to himself, and cut into his steak.

"What's that?" Shane asked.

"I'm saying that it seems to be *our* business when we're about to sell. It was *my* business when all the bills had to be paid."

"It's *our* business. We had a deal." Shane slid the plate away in disgust and lit up another cigarette.

"We wouldn't have to sell at all if you weren't fucking his wife," Curt muttered.

Shane heard that one. "You're selling up because you're a terrible promoter. You had a gift in me down here. I was a fucking star and you're dithering."

"Dithering?"

"Yeah, fucking dithering."

"Is that even a word?" Curt asked.

"Yes, it's a word. What do you mean is it a word? Did you hear it come out of my ass? No? It came from my brain, out my mouth. It's a fucking word then."

"Okay. It's a word."

Shane reset his thoughts to the matter at hand and tried again. "You've been too soft for the last two years. Waiting on Danno's good graces. You should have pulled on him harder."

Curt banged his fork handle on the table. "I could have had a golden ring with money falling out of the ceiling down here and

Danno wasn't going to do business with me. It had nothing to do with my skills. I asked you. I asked you when we were putting this deal together if there was anything I should know."

"Yeah? And?"

"And? And? You were fucking the man's wife."

Shane felt a little trapped by that reality. "How was I supposed to know *he* knew that? Did you want me to ask him? Did you want me to check with Danno to see if he knew that I was boning his sweetheart before I signed with you?"

Curt slid his plate away too. "I can't wait to get out of this fucking business. I've lost my house, my company, my wife, my kids. And then I have you putting a gun to my fucking head to pay you on a contract that we shook on years ago. I couldn't make the match. You know that. You saw what Danno was like. Fucking intent on making sure that match between you and Babu didn't happen. Why are you—"

Shane leaned in good and close. He had a terrified wife waiting for him, and a kid in shock, refusing to speak. He had some very serious men looking to track him down. He just wasn't in the mood to patter back and forth about who was further up shit creek.

"I gave you time," Shane said very deliberately. "I took money from people I shouldn't have, just to feed my family because of your good word—"

"You took money to fuck, gamble, and fly around like Mr. Millionaire. My family home was sold so you could shove it up your nose," Curt said.

Shane continued at a deliberate pace. "On your word. On your word I got that money loaned to me. It doesn't fucking matter what I did with it." He slid his chair back and stood up. "Make this right tomorrow. I haven't got any more time left to dodge these people. Because I promise that if you try to fuck me over with the payoff, I will make sure that whatever happens to my family happens ten times back to yours."

Shane pulled his collar up.

"That's right, leave me to handle one last bill, you prick," Curt said as he watched Shane leave.

October 9, 1972.
The day of Annie's murder.
Texas.

He had been everywhere and dined with everyone. He had ridden in the best transportation the world had to offer. He wore the finest clothes money could buy. He became successful in his life without being able to read or write to any large degree. There was nothing decadent on earth that he hadn't fucked, eaten, smoked, snorted, or bought. But this day, Shane Montrose woke in the back of a broken-down secondhand hatchback on the side of an unknown Texas road.

He opened the door and fell out onto the dusty ground. The sun focused right on the top of his head, which made him sick and dizzy. He stood with his dick in his hand and willed it to work. Just a little. Just a trickle. Anything. Where one part of his body refused to discharge fluid, another, his mouth, was more helpful. He had nothing solid in his stomach to produce, so a swirl of acidic bile projected from his lips and darkened the dust around his feet. He didn't even bother to try to avoid it. He just stood there with his dick in his hand, puking stomach water all over himself. His shoes, his leisure suit ruined—or *more* ruined. His pockets empty. His family was terrified and he felt he was just a couple of hours away from ending up on the underside of the dust below his feet. His stomach quickly and violently heaved and pulled him in the opposite direction. He struggled to open his belt in time and squat. No paper either.

"Fuck," he said with absolutely no conviction.

He was too beat. Too tired. Too hung over. Too jittery. So, somewhere in Texas, he halfheartedly shit.

Curt walked into the hotel bar. He knew today was the day that he would make the deal to get the fuck out of the wrestling

business. The time was right. On top of the hardship that natu-
rally came with being a boss, Curt also knew that Danno had
been paying his local TV station double just to keep Curt's wrestling show off the air. Danno was essentially, and effectively,
killing Curt's Texas territory from New York—without starting
another war.

But Curt knew Danno wasn't having it all his own way either.
He listened with delight while Tanner Blackwell told him over the
phone how Danno had just fucked up the biggest match of all time
in Shea Stadium. Neither Babu or the challenger Danno went with
instead of Sugarstick showed up to the event. Such misery should
have brought a great smile to Curt's face. But all he could think of
was that if Danno had just listened to him and his proposal for a
main event, everything would have been all right. They both would
have been rich. Instead, now they were scheduled to meet in Texas
so Danno could pay him bottom dollar for his wrestling company
that hadn't functioned properly in years. Either way, Curt was just
happy to be able to get enough money to pay his debts and break out
of it with a couple of grand for himself. All he had to do was get the
money before Shane Montrose found him. And then hide so Shane
Montrose couldn't find him.

Shane was past the point of giving a fuck about anything. He had
traveled a couple of miles down the road and was standing in a
musty phone box just outside a tiny town he didn't recognize.

His vomit was drying into his clothes, he was sucking on a raw bottle of vodka, and he had a white powdery ring around his left nostril.

"Hello?" Shane said belligerently to the answering voice.

"Who's this?" Grobie asked from the other end of the line.

Shane had been expecting Curt. "Sorry, Grobie. It's the Sugarstick
here. I was looking for Curt."

"He should be there by now," she replied, sounding slightly confused. "He left here about fifteen minutes ago."

Shane knew she was getting her wires crossed somewhere, but played along. "He left already?"

"Yeah, unless he stopped somewhere for gas or something," she replied.

"Okay," Shane said, unable to think of a way to reply properly.

He was about to hang up and try to digest what he'd just heard when Grobie chimed back in again. "Are you two coming back here to celebrate after? I can roast you a chicken or something."

Shane was trying to figure out what was going on.

"You could come by yourself anytime. You know that, right?" she asked.

"What? Yeah. Of course."

Shane's broken brain pieced together the scant information. A meeting happening now, fifteen minutes from Grobie's house. He needed more.

"Maybe we could bring back a bottle from here?" he asked, totally unsure of her potential answer.

"That would be perfect," she said.

"Listen . . . you wouldn't know the name of the place? I've got a little hangover here and I'm blanking on the name."

There was a pause on the line.

"Grobie?" he said. "I know it's something, something . . ."

"I have to go," she said.

"Wait."

She hung up.

Shane ran back to his shitty car. Whatever was going down, it was happening right now, and he wasn't even sure how far from the meeting point he was.

Annie made her way down to the hotel bar carrying the rucksack full of money. This was what she wanted, a piece of business to handle to help her husband get through this. The bar was quiet and mostly empty. She looked out for a man her husband had described as "a really brown fuck, with a white mustache and shaky hands."

Annie scrutinized the room and ordered a drink. Curt sat by the window and kept a nervous eye out for Shane Montrose. The last thing he needed was him showing up and embarrassing, or derailing, the deal.

"Curt?" Annie asked.

"Yes?" Curt answered, a little confused.

Annie Garland offered a handshake and Curt obliged while standing up.

"Hello. I'm Annie Garland. I think we met briefly in New York at a party," she said as she sat down at the table.

Curt thought that maybe Annie was in town with Danno and was just saying hello on her way through. "Oh yes, Mrs. Garland. Your anniversary party. I'm sorry; I wasn't expecting to see you down here. I was in a world of my own. Has your husband been delayed?"

"He's not coming," Annie answered.

Curt's stomach sank. "Excuse me?"

"As you may know, my husband is otherwise engaged tonight. Although he is anxious to complete the deal before the main event begins later in Florida."

Curt couldn't believe that Danno would disrespect him again. He stood up. "I'm sorry, darling, but this is a slap in the face to me and a waste of my fucking time."

"Sit down, Mr. Magee, or the deal will be pulled immediately," Annie said while opening the rucksack. She noticed an envelope on top that said 'Sorry' in someone's handwriting.

"Excuse me?" Curt said.

Annie was distracted. It wasn't Danno's writing and she had no idea why such a thing would be in the bag. She quickly composed herself and got back to the business at hand. "I said there will be no second go-around here today or any other day, Mr. Magee. My husband's offer expires the second you leave this bar."

Curt struggled to contain his contempt for the power this woman seemed to have over him. "What's going on here? I thought we had a deal. I have a line of people who are looking for payments from me, Mrs. Garland. I told your husband that going out of business is not a cheap pursuit."

Curt couldn't resist looking out the window to make sure the number-one person in his debtor line hadn't figured out where he was.

"We want to do a deal," Annie said. "I came all the way down here to make sure that happens."

Curt knew he didn't have time to grandstand. He could only sit back into his seat like a lobster being eased into a pot. "And Danno gave you full permission to make the decisions to get this deal done?" Curt asked.

Annie, still intrigued by the envelope, opened it under the table. Inside there were two ladies' rings. One looked to be an engagement ring and the other a wedding ring.

"I don't want to prolong this humiliation any further, Mrs. Garland. Your husband promised me a cash deal here today." Curt's nerves were beginning to show on his face. It looked to Annie like both of his hands were shaking now.

Annie quickly pocketed the rings and read the note that accompanied them: I'M SORRY BOSS. I DON'T HAVE ALL THE MONEY. I WILL PAY YOU BACK. I PROMISE. I'M SORRY. LENNY.

"Is there a problem?" Curt asked, starting to get nervous and a little paranoid about what Annie was silently reading under the table.

Annie knew now she didn't have the money to make the deal. At a bar in Texas, Annie and Curt were both starting to feel the pressure of this deal.

Shane crisscrossed all the bars and restaurants within fifteen minutes of Grobie's house. He knew the ones Curt liked to drink in, but there was no sign of him.

He waited for the red lights to turn green. Another opportunity to burn through some coke. He tried to focus on what he knew. Curt wasn't going to bring Danno to a shitty bar. He was going to try and impress him, make Danno think that he was a big-shot owner. There weren't that many options to choose from and Shane Montrose knew every expensive bar, club, and hotel in Texas. It was there, under the red light, that he knew exactly where Curt was.

Annie counted the remaining blocks of cash in a stall of the ladies room. Eighty-four thousand. Saying she had eighty-four thousand made her look like an amateur. A round, concise number conveyed the confidence that she was acting from. She composed herself and packed seventy back into the rucksack. She crammed the rest into her purse.

Out in the bar, Curt was still waiting at the table. That alone led Annie to believe that this deal wasn't dead.

He looked twitchy and constantly scanned the room.

"My apologies, Curt. Had to . . ."

Curt was far past Annie's faux charm. "I want a hundred and twenty thousand now, Mrs. Garland. Your husband's disrespect toward me has been shocking and upsetting, quite frankly. He and I have served together on the National Wrestling Council for . . ."

Annie stopped him dead by raising her hand in his direction. She couldn't show weakness and she couldn't let herself be pushed around. "I'm going to give you seventy thousand now, Curt. You get less for being an asshole to me."

"The original deal was for ninety thousand," he said.

"And you've just tried to hold me up for an extra thirty grand on top of that," she replied. "So I'm cutting our offer by twenty grand."

Curt laughed. "This is why I don't deal with the wives, Mrs. Garland. They are crazy one hundred percent of the time."

Annie fired back, "If you disrespect me one more time, I will pull the money from this deal altogether."

Shane pulled his dying car into a spot at the edge of the parking lot. He surveyed the area and spotted Curt's car parked around the side of the hotel, away from prying eyes. He knew he was being cut out of a deal again. A deal that could save his life; that could save his family's lives. Shane was too old not to collect on every penny his broken-down body could make for him, and deals like the one he signed with Curt Magee would never come around for him again.

Shane Montrose wanted what was his.

He left his car and stooped and staggered underneath the windows of the hotel bar. He wanted to scout the get-together and see what was happening. He cowered behind a parked truck and took stock of the patrons through the window. Inside, he could see Curt's back but not much past him.

He moved again to try to get a better angle but he was drawn to the slap of the bar door closing. He saw Curt hurrying toward his car, but he veered off at the last second to the parking lot pay phone instead. Shane wondered what had got Curt so annoyed. He peered back in the window and the sight of Annie Garland beyond the glass hotel door stopped him dead in his tracks.

Shane knelt back down again, almost unable to take in what he was seeing. His head was scrambled enough, but he never thought in a million years that Annie would be in a deal to fuck him over. But nothing surprised him in the wrestling business.

Fucking bitch.

She walked out and went quickly up the outside steps to her room on the second floor.

From the pay phone Curt watched Annie go to her room. He tried calling Danno but got the machine instead: "Hello, you have reached the New York Booking Agency, the home of the world's greatest wrestling attractions. We are unable to come to the phone right now so please leave a message. Thank you."

Beep.

Curt slammed the phone on the glass before taking his phone book from his pocket and dialing again. Another answering machine. This time with no message. It was Danno's home number.

Beep.

Curt didn't even know where to start. "Danno," he blurted out. "You fucking fat piece of shit. Sending your fucking wife down was an insult. You know that, Danno? She's a fucking whore. Who do you think you are trying to stiff me at the last minute? You bring down the money we agreed. That was the deal. Not some light fucking number you made up. The deal. You made a deal."

Danno's offer, Danno's wife, and Danno squeezing him out of the business made Curt feel small-time. On his own. Isolated was a bad place to be in the wrestling business. "And if you think I'm going to take this lying down . . . well, fuck you."

Curt slammed the phone down.

Shane watched Curt get into his car and roar off. He had no idea what to think. He couldn't figure out what the angle was.

Who was fucking who?

Seeing Annie Garland walk from the lobby and hurry to her room made him think it was *him* who was taking it in the ass. He expected the fucking promoters to backstab him and try to slit his throat, but the woman who told him she loved him? He never saw that coming.

She was in on it all along, he thought. *That fucking bitch was in it all along.*

A quarter mile down the road, Curt Magee could hardly control his anger. He was shaking with adrenaline and his mind was wild with scenes of Danno, and maybe even the other bosses, laughing at him. He couldn't go home empty-handed. He wouldn't go home empty-handed. Curt slammed on the brakes and turned his car around.

He was going to teach Danno a lesson.

October 11, 1972.
Five days after Annie's murder.
Texas.

Curt was restless in the dark. For days he had woken up with the feeling that he could go back to the way it was, could make all this better. He could do things differently. He hated being on the run. He just wanted out of this fucking business for good. He rolled from his right hip onto his left and punched his pillow into comfort. A chill ran along his spine as he sensed someone else in the room with him. His eyes shot open and he could see a hooded Shane Montrose kneeling at the head of his bed.

"What the fuck are you—" Curt tried to ask before Shane lunged forward, grabbed Curt's mouth, and drove a kitchen knife into his neck. Curt instinctively held his neck but blood escaped freely between his fingers.

"I saw the fucking money in her room. I know what you were trying to do to me," Shane whispered as Curt choked on his own blood.

It didn't matter how many times Shane had visualized Curt dying, or how many times he imagined what that might be like, it was horrifying to see it happen in front of him. It was the way Curt stared at him as he fought to breathe; the look of terror on his face as he knew he was dying.

"My fucking family are hiding, afraid for their lives . . ." Shane said weakly.

Curt fought to sit up, to change his position, to try to pull in a small breath of air. Shane grabbed him by the head and pulled a pillow tight over Curt's face. Curt kicked the walls, grabbed around with his hands, and made guttural noises too loud to contain. It was supposed to be easier than this. Quicker. Cleaner. This wasn't the way dying happened on TV. Curt's fight was going to get Shane caught—and Shane was way too far in now to go back.

"I can't have you talking out there, Curt. I can't . . ." Shane hysterically began to hack at Curt's neck and face under the pillow. Knife in; knife out. In. Out. In. Out. In again. Over and over. The pillow became soggy and blood soaked as he punctured Curt's flesh again and again. Shane was stabbing at any piece of skin or flesh he could see—chest, stomach, arms. He just wanted Curt to stop fighting.

Die. Die. Die. Fucking die.

Shane dropped his knife and furiously punched Curt in the face over and over. His thoughts became words with every strike. "Fucking die. Fucking die. Fucking die, you . . . fucking die."

And then nothing. No fight. No struggle. Curt went limp. The only sound Shane could hear was the sound of a baby crying behind him. He turned to see Grobie, in the doorway of the room opposite, paralyzed with fear. She had her hand across her baby's mouth trying to keep his cries quiet.

Shane jumped up and ran past her, taking the stairs too many steps at a time. He stumbled, tripped, and fell to the bottom. The baby upstairs screamed with fright. Shane felt his forearm snap when he hit the last step. He clambered to his feet. He dragged himself along the hallway and into the kitchen. He swung open the back door and knew straightaway that he couldn't climb that hedge again—especially with a newly broken arm.

He changed direction and limped along the side of the house and out onto the street.

CHAPTER FOURTEEN

October 9, 1972.
The day of Annie's murder.
Texas.

Curt's car came roaring into the parking lot. He pulled into a free parking spot and launched himself from his seat. He walked to the window of the bar in the hotel to make sure she wasn't in there. He quickly checked the lobby too. No sign. She must have still been in her room.

He hurried up the outside steps to where Annie was staying. He didn't know what he was going to do, but he was going to make sure that no one took him for a fucking pushover again. If today was Curt's last day in the wrestling business, he was going to make sure that each and every one of the other bosses would remember him for a long time to come.

He walked up to Annie's door and pounded on it as hard as he could. He knew there was no way she was going to answer it. So he tried to bust his way in.

"Annie," he shouted with his forehead on the door. "You let me in."

Curt's aggression and volume caught the attention of some of the other hotel patrons.

Annie's room was quiet. He could hear nothing inside. He checked to make sure he had the right door. It was definitely the one he had seen her enter earlier. Maybe she had checked out already. Maybe she had made a run for it. Curt scrutinized the parking lot for movement or anything suspicious. He had one last quick look around and threw a kick at the door. His heart was pumping and he was having a hard time un-balling his fists.

"Annie?" he shouted as he kicked again. The door shot open. Curt saw Annie lying on the floor, dead.

He backed out slowly, turned, and ran for his life down the steps and toward his car. People in other rooms watched him flee from their windows.

October 10, 1972.
Five minutes before Annie's murder.
Texas.

Annie Garland collected the few things she had and threw them into her bag. She didn't know what she was going to tell her husband. She had made a huge mess of the one deal he ever trusted her with. As cool as she had played it with Curt, she now feared for her safety in Texas. Annie wasn't used to the type of anger that she saw at the end of their meeting. She was sure her husband could pull something together in the end, but she had wanted to close the deal herself.

She took out two pills and lay them in her cupped hand before downing them with a drink of water. She felt the rings and note in her pocket. Annie thought she would bring the rings back home and quietly return them to Lenny. Danno didn't have to know.

"Annie?" whispered a familiar voice from outside the door.

Even his voice made her feel a certain way. It was a way she had a hard time explaining, but that instantly attracted her. Through the fisheye in her door, she saw a distorted version of Shane Montrose outside. She cracked the door open and let him in. He looked disheveled and clearly needed a shower. His clothes were stained and his eyes were red and raw. Annie had never really seen him like this before.

"What are you doing here?" she asked.

"What are *you* doing here?" he asked in return. His version of the question sounded loaded and paranoid.

Annie took seriously the instructions to not let anyone know about the deal. It wasn't to be announced to anyone in case one of the other bosses swooped in and picked over the bones of Curtis's territory for a quarter of the price.

"I was just . . . visiting a friend. A girlfriend from college."

Shane approached her too quickly and too aggressively for her liking. "I fucking saw you out there with him," Shane said. His teeth were clenched and his eyes were saucer wide. Annie had seen a fraction of this before. She had seen him go wild. He would punch something and flex his muscles. Get into a brawl. Ten minutes later he would hold her gently to his chest and try to explain why he did what he did. He always failed to put into words why he acted like that, but a man like Shane Montrose got very good at learning how to apologize the right way.

He grabbed her wrists. "Answer me, Annie. What are you doing down here?" he shouted as he kicked the door closed behind him.

"It's none of your business what I do," she said as she struggled free. "What right have you got to ask me anything like that?"

"You're in on this with them, aren't you?"

"What?"

"Your fat fuck of a husband is pulling you back in, isn't he?"

Annie walked to the door but Shane stood in her path. "I want you to leave. Now," she said, her voice rising with fright. Annie turned her back on him and he grabbed her hair and yanked her onto the bed.

"Were you in on this from the start? Were you part of them cutting me out of this?" Shane followed her eyes as she instinctively looked toward the bag full of money. He could make out the faintest sight of the bills on top.

They both dived for the bag and grabbed a handle each. Annie refused to let go.

"That's my fucking money," he shouted and lashed out, slapping her across the face.

They both paused in shock, her face stinging from the impact of his hand. She had never been hit before. Annie rose to her feet and walked quickly for the door.

"I'm sorry," he pleaded. He couldn't let her go. He needed to make it right before she got back to Danno. Money and backstabbing was all fair play. But hitting the boss's wife? That would get you killed.

"Annie?" He walked into her path again. Her right cheek was red and there were tears coming to her eyes. "They are going to kill my family, Annie. Please."

"Move," she said, trying not to cry in front of him.

"My little girl. I have to get the money. They've been to my house."

Annie wasn't listening. Or didn't care anymore. Either way, Shane knew if she crossed that door he was dead.

He grabbed her from behind, pulled her back forcefully onto the bed, cranked his arm under her chin, and clasped his hands shut. She struggled a little in silence but the strength of his grip around her neck left her helpless. She could only kick her legs and try in vain to unlock his hands.

They both lay on her bed. They both knew she was dying. They both waited for it to happen. They both cried. Her body was unresponsive but her mind knew exactly what was happening. She violently jerked and tried one last time to free herself. To breathe. To run for the door. To see her husband. Then she went limp. He let her go and guided her sliding body softly onto the floor.

He wiped his eyes and looked at her. He was in shock at what he had done; what he was capable of doing. She was gone and there was no way he could reverse it. Make it better. Make it different.

The sound of a car roaring into the parking lot snapped him back to his new reality.

Shane shook the money from Annie's purse, stacked it on top of the money in the rucksack, secured it all, and left the room.

CHAPTER FIFTEEN

October 11, 1972.
Five days after Annie's murder.
Texas.

Mickey Jack turned onto Grobie's street and immediately saw the ambulances and police cars. Their lights were flashing in the dark and people were gathered outside to see what was happening.

"Just continue, I have the wrong place," Mickey Jack said to his cab driver. He double-checked the address he got from Danno; this was the house for sure.

Mickey seemed to have a knack for turning up with the job already done. As he passed, he snuck a look through the back window and could see a covered body being wheeled out of the house. A local news truck was also unloading its equipment as the cab turned the corner, taking him out of sight.

"Where to now?" the cab driver asked.

"Take me back to the airport," Mickey said, sliding a five dollar bill between the front seats.

October 12, 1972.
Six days after Annie's murder.
New York.

Joe Lapine never fucking liked the phone ringing when he was asleep.

That stupid fucking phone, fucking ringing and giving me a fucking heart attack.

"What?" he shouted down the line.

"Are you on your own?" Tanner Blackwell asked in a very matter-of-fact way.

Joe threw the phone on the bed and begrudgingly put on his glasses. Ten seconds in, and he already knew this was going to be a terrible fucking day. He rose and fumbled around for the light switch. It was late afternoon but ceiling-to-floor heavy curtains blocked out the daylight. Just as he liked it.

"Move it," he grunted to the woman in his bed. She didn't move nearly fast enough out of the room.

"Chop, chop, sweetheart," he said as he stomped around clapping his hands like he was trying to scare chickens out of his path.

With the room now empty and the curtains pulled back, Joe sat on the edge of his bed.

"You there, Joe?" Tanner shouted.

Joe picked up the phone and put it to his ear. "Yeah?"

"I just got a phone call from Texas. Un-fucking-believable. We have to settle this now," Tanner said.

Across town, Ricky was nodding off in his chair while Ginny took a bath. Ricky kind of enjoyed not having to talk sometimes, so he'd put on something loud and distracting. Something hard to talk over. He liked his day after a Garden card to be peaceful—an all too infrequent thing these days.

Joe sat with his head in his hands in his hotel room chair.

"So, one of the wrestlers Curt fucked over on a payoff called one of my guys, who called me," Tanner said, explaining how he knew what he knew.

"Are you sure it's Curt?" Joe asked.

Tanner was getting annoyed at how little of a fuck his chairman seemed to give. "Yes, it's all over the TV down there. His goddamn girlfriend gave an eyewitness account that it was Shane-fucking-Montrose they were looking for."

Tanner paused and then his voice went cold. "Just tell me that you're fixing this now. We warned Garland to stay away from Texas."

"How do you know Danno was behind this?" Joe asked.

"Don't give me that shit, Joe. You know what has to happen here. I need to be protected. I'm fucking in with Danno and the title situation up to my ass now."

Joe was genuinely hurt by what he was about to do. "I got it," he said.

"You've got an hour," Tanner warned him. "You handle it within an hour—or I do."

"I fucking got it," Joe snapped as he slammed the phone down.

In that instant, Joe Lapine from Memphis, Tennessee, found himself tasked with the job of protecting the wrestling business and making sure it sustained no more damage. He was left with zero options. Danno was making Joe deal with him. He was making him do something he didn't want to do. For nearly a hundred years the wrestling business had kept its mouth shut, put its head down and just made money. Joe knew that they couldn't let one man—Danno Garland—ruin all that. So he quickly got dressed and made his way to the hotel hallway, where last night's date was sitting patiently on the floor outside his door.

"So what do I tell my husband?" the young woman asked as she stood quickly.

Joe was on the move. "Tell him to call my office in a couple of days."

"You're going to hire him? He could be a champion, I'm telling you."

Joe ignored her and entered the elevator. *Ding.* He walked out onto the marble floor and across the nearly empty lobby, through the large revolving door, and out into the New York hustle, where he found a pay phone on the corner. He took a small book from his back pocket and flipped through the pages as the city pushed and pulled its inhabitants up and down the blocks. He dialed a number and waited a few rings until the voice kicked in, "Hello, you have reached the New York Booking Agency, the home—"

Joe hung up and quickly went to his book again. He dialed. The chairman needed to deal with the issue or he in turn would be dealt with.

"Hello?" answered the voice on the other end of the line. It was Ricky.

"Hello," Joe replied.

"Joe?" Ricky asked. "What's wrong?"

Joe heard Ricky's TV blaring in the background. "You got a big fucking problem here. You want to turn that down?" Joe asked.

"What problem?" Ricky asked.

Joe didn't even know where to start. But he knew he didn't have time to sugarcoat anything. "Curt was killed. It was down in Texas and they've got Shane Montrose."

Ricky's day off was ruined. "It was Shane?"

"I was hoping *you* could tell *me*," Joe snapped back.

Ricky was genuinely confused. "What?"

"What's he gone and done, Ricky?" Joe asked. "I can't protect him no more."

"I don't know. I don't know what he's doing out there anymore," Ricky said honestly. He was tired of defending Danno. The whole business had heard Danno put a bounty on Curt Magee. Ricky couldn't make this one better. What was left that he could do?

"I can tell you what's coming next," Joe said. "Tanner is going to set the cops on him."

Joe felt like he was betraying another boss by talking to Ricky and giving him a heads-up. But he liked Danno and appreciated Danno giving him the chairman position.

"Why?" Ricky asked. "What does that do?"

Joe said, "He knows Danno is where all the poison is coming from. He wants to serve him up, make him the reason for all this stuff, and make all this go away in one fell swoop."

Ricky tried to interrupt but Joe stopped him. "Danno's finished. I'm sorry," Joe said. "I wanted you to hear it from me. I have no other choice but to back Tanner in getting rid of Danno. No other fucking choice, Ricky."

Ricky needed more time to think. He had never come across a situation where someone from within the NWC was talking about ratting another boss to the cops. Ricky wondered whether Mickey Jack Crisp was trustworthy. He wondered if Mickey had done what he paid him to do.

"What's he going to say, Joe? I need to know what's coming," Ricky said.

"Don't waste time trying to fix this. Tell Danno to run and get the fuck out yourself if you can," Joe replied.

"What's he going to say?" Ricky asked more forcefully.

"Ricky? I swear to God . . . don't you try and fix—"

Ricky slammed down the phone and bolted from his apartment.

Joe put his phone down and watched as New York struggled past outside. It was dirty, noisy, and packed with panhandlers, whores, and junkies. He wanted to go home to Tennessee where he could breathe clean air.

New York was nothing but a fucking headache.

Danno waited by the phone, fully dressed with his shoes still tied. He had been sitting there in his house all night and all day wondering when Mickey Jack Crisp was going to call from Texas. Danno used the empty time to imagine what it would be like to pump a bullet into the man who killed his wife. Mickey would hold Curt somewhere in Texas; Danno would show up and kill him. He would return home, put on the suit he had laid out on his bed, take his gun, put it to his own head, and follow his wife.

But with no one around, and his thoughts all to himself, Danno knew that having to kill again sickened and frightened him. But what else could he do? How else could he begin to make it right? Not doing anything was even harder than doing something. And that's where he found himself, with no real good option. Danno only had the terrible choice of killing again or the unbearable choice of not.

The shrill sound of his phone finally ringing jumped him out of his thoughts.

"Hello?" he said hurriedly.

"It's me," Mickey answered.

"Where the fuck were you?" Danno snapped.

"It's not a good situation down here."

"Have you got him?" Danno asked.

Mickey paused as he tried to figure out what to say next.

"What is it?" Danno asked.

"Do you want to make your way to another phone and call me back or something?" Mickey asked.

Danno didn't care. "No."

Mickey drew a couple of pained breaths and stuttered his way into a poorly constructed line. "I don't know . . ."

Danno could wait no longer. "Fucking say it."

"Curt is dead," Mickey said.

"What did you do?" Danno shouted angrily.

"Not me. They're saying on the news that they're holding Shane Montrose in connection to it."

"What?" Danno asked in disbelief.

"I'm watching the local news down here. Shane Montrose. They've got a picture of him up on the screen now. They arrested him a couple of miles from the house."

Danno couldn't process what he was hearing. How did Shane get down there? How did he know where Curt was?

"I got to go," Mickey said.

"Wait."

"What?"

"He's dead?" Danno asked disbelievingly.

"Yeah." Mickey hung up.

Danno sat with the phone to his ear and tried to digest what had happened. A sneaking feeling of relief came over him. He couldn't stop it, even though he was ashamed of feeling that way.

It was over.

He could now put on his suit and put himself out of his misery.

He stood and moved toward his staircase. As he took the first step he heard a car approaching on his gravel driveway outside. Danno quickly checked the corner of his window before taking up residence behind his front door. He saw headlights but the darkness outside wouldn't allow him to see who it was. With Curt dead, and the way he died, Danno wasn't sure if the car was coming for him next. If Danno was going to die that night, he was going to die his own way.

He heard the car engine stop and saw the shine of headlights dim through the glass. As the footsteps approached, he reached for his gun.

Maybe it wasn't over yet.

The visitor rang the bell. Danno took some shallow breaths and waited for their next move.

"Hello? You there? Boss?" Lenny shouted.

Lenny?

Danno took another quick look through the glass before opening the door. Lenny was standing there smiling.

"I . . . knew you were here," Lenny blurted out.

Danno couldn't help but smile back at seeing the harmless Lenny Long standing in front of him.

"I just wanted to say hello," Lenny said as he walked cautiously toward his former boss. He had Danno's missing money in the back of his car. Money Lenny wanted to trade for his wife's rings back. It was important to Lenny that Bree have what he gave her when he asked her to be his wife.

"How are things here?" Lenny asked.

Danno dropped his head a little when he felt his lip quiver. He put out his arms and Lenny, totally confused as to what was happening, moved quicker into Danno's embrace. "I'm so happy to see you," Danno said sincerely. "I'm so happy you're okay."

Danno compressed Lenny's slight frame and lifted him off the ground. Lenny could see his boss was far happier to see him now than he ever had been when he worked for him.

"I thought you were dead," Danno said holding Lenny at arm's length. "I thought . . ." Danno became emotional. But he stopped himself from crying.

"I'm not dead, boss. I should have said something to you. I was going to call when we got settled. Me and the family . . ."

Danno didn't care. He just wanted another hug.

Texas.

Mickey Jack Crisp stood in the Dallas Airport with more money than he knew what to do with. He could maybe go home to Florida and set up something. A little business, or use the money for a deposit on a house or something. He would more than likely use it for no good. Maybe get some girls. Definitely get some girls.

"Whatever you have left will be fine," Mickey Jack said at the airport rent-a-car desk. "And gimme a full tank."

Danno's chartered plane waited on the runway outside to take Mickey back to New York, but Mickey just wanted to get back home. He didn't want to get any further in with the wrestling guys. They were all at war and it was hard for Mickey to know which horse to back in that race. He had cash stuffed and taped all over his body. A rental car would be easier. A day or two to Gainesville, then he could fade into obscurity as he made his way down home.

Mickey Jack Crisp had earned his money; he had done what he was paid to do.

Kinda.

CHAPTER SIXTEEN

New York.

Troy Bartlett spent four days in various holding cages. He was moved constantly from precinct to precinct and kept in the dark as to why he had been picked up—or what they were holding him for. Although, even with all the dodgy clients he had, and all the shady deals he'd made, Troy knew it was because he was Danno Garland's lawyer.

For the first couple of days he tried threatening the cops. But he knew they didn't give a fuck about the law. Then he tried reasoning. Then he gave up and just sat there, wondering, trying to piece together what was going on. From one shitty green-walled precinct to another. There was the constant sound of filing cabinets opening and closing, typewriters being pecked at, phones ringing, cars starting and parking outside. Each time, all they'd tell Troy was there was no room for him in whatever division and he would be moved again. Precinct to precinct, with nobody talking.

But he knew it was connected to Danno.

Troy had been around enough departments, heard enough stories, and paid into enough illegal envelopes to know what the bent cops looked like.

He had known he was being tailed long before they picked him up.

Particularly when it was business to do with Danno. Troy hoped the tail would go when Danno's Senate hearing was over. He was wrong.

Katy Spence stood outside Troy's new holding cage. She was dressed in full police uniform.

"How are you today, Troy?" she asked as she dragged a chair into position and sat down.

Troy had had enough. He owed nobody nothing in this world. Not even Danno Garland. He had been tight-lipped for days but he wasn't made for this. He was a meticulous man who couldn't abide imposition. He wasn't street tough and didn't want to be. He was paid to be a different kind of hard. A type of hard that he knew one day could end him up exactly where he was.

"I last spoke to Danno Garland less than two weeks ago. On October first," he said without much prompting.

Katy was taken a little off guard by Troy's candor. After days of resistance, maybe he had simply been stewing for long enough.

Troy continued. "It was the day before the Senate hearings. He didn't know how it was going to go. He didn't know what was going to happen. He was stashing all his cash in bags and running around his house packing up valuables."

"And what did you talk about?" Katy asked. She felt slightly out of her depth, but she didn't want Troy to stop now that he started.

"I need to get out of here," Troy said. "I think I'm losing my fucking mind."

"I can arrange your release after a few more questions," Katy replied.

In an ordinary case moving in an ordinary direction, there would be no way a rookie like Katy would be let near a witness. But Katy wasn't taking orders in the normal way. Danno Garland didn't know his lawyer was in police custody, but neither did Captain Miller. This one was totally off the books, for now.

"The last piece of business I had with Danno was a preemptive and hasty meeting in the barn beside his house," Troy said. "He wanted to move his businesses out of his own name just in case the government decided to go after him."

"Tell me what happened," Katy said.

She could see that Troy didn't trust her one bit.

"I can just leave if you'd like," she said. "Come back tomorrow."

She stood slowly to give him time to change his mind. She pushed her seat back against the wall and turned off the lights.'

"He was hiding money," Troy said. "Wrapped in the bales of hay. Shouting for his wife. We met in the barn."

Katy turned back on the light and walked closer to the cage. "What did you meet him for?"

"He wanted to sign over his assets. I'm his lawyer," Troy said. "Nothing illegal. Nothing going on."

"Why would a guy sign over anything?"

"He was nervous that the government was going to get him because of the hearings. Again," Troy said, getting more frustrated at his situation. "Nothing fucking illegal."

"To his wife?" Katy asked.

Troy slowly shook his head. "No. He didn't trust her. Thought she was running around behind his back."

"So who did he sign the business over to?" Katy asked.

Troy thought about how he was to answer. He wanted out of the cell in the worst way. He had come to feel a certain loyalty to Danno over the years. But here he was, cell number four, and there was no knight on a white horse breaking down the door to rescue him. He always knew that the wrestling business was cutthroat. He just didn't think that he was far enough in to have to worry about it.

"Mr. Bartlett?" Katy asked again. "Who did Danno Garland sign his assets over to?"

Troy knew his only way out of this shit was to tell her.

CHAPTER SEVENTEEN

The First Precinct was small, too small for the amount of work that the city, under pressure, was throwing at it. Inside stood the large booking desk, a fleet of filing cabinets, a couple of hand-marked doors, and Captain Miller waiting alone by the restrooms.

His quiet demeanor made all the other cops working around him anxious. They pantomimed their work a little more to show him how hard they were trying. A couple of new officers even admonished a suspect in front of him and then dragged him away, thinking that's what Matthew Miller liked.

They were wrong.

He was only sitting there for one reason. And that reason had just walked in the door.

"You," Miller said to Nestor. "In here."

The captain stood and walked into the vacant interview room beside him. Nestor took off his coat and shook off the rain. He watched as the other cops could hardly hold their delight at someone, anyone, getting called in to be yelled at. At least that's what looked like was going to happen. Nestor thought for a fleeting second about walking past the open door and continuing on his way upstairs to his desk. He didn't have time for any of this bullshit. But he still marched into the room like a kid going to see the principal.

"Close the door," the captain ordered.

Nestor closed the door. Through the blind he could see the rapid exchange of information between his colleagues as to what they thought was happening.

"Sit down."

Nestor sat down.

"What happened with Danno Garland last night?" the captain asked.

"I don't know," Nestor answered.

"Two uniforms picked him up at the airport. They said that you were involved."

"Cooper?" Nestor asked.

Miller barely nodded in response.

Nestor seemed annoyed that he even had to explain. "That asshole picked up Garland for nothing. If we're going to get something on him, we have to make sure that it's something that's going to stick."

"And what's that got to do with you, one way or the other?" the captain asked.

Nestor took a split second too long to answer. "Because of the conversation that you and I had in your office the other day. I wanted to see if there was anything to what you were saying. Help you out."

The captain slipped his hands in his pockets and rocked backwards and forwards on his heels. Nestor recognized this as *Irish Cop Confidence 101.*

"You were just helping your captain out?" Miller asked.

"Doing my job. Sir."

The captain saw a little too much attitude coming from Nestor. "You're a liar," he said bluntly.

"What?"

"You're lying to me. And I fucking won't have it."

"Are you accusing me of—"

Miller cut Nestor off. "You're damn right I am. You're holding back on me about this man. You know things. You have a handle on what's going on out there with him and his crew. And you're still not telling me. And that leads me to think things I shouldn't be thinking."

"Not true," Nestor said.

"Not true?"

"Do you want me to talk honestly in here?"

The captain nodded. "'Bout fucking time."

"This precinct is dirty. I don't like Cooper for that very reason. He was the wrong fucking person to pick someone like Danno Garland up. You know what I'm saying? So what I do is keep my cases, leads, and anything else to myself . . ."

The emergence of a silhouette outside the blind stopped the conversation's momentum. The figure knocked on the door. Neither man inside moved to answer it, so the waiting officer knocked again.

"Yeah?" Miller snapped.

A slightly nervous officer opened the door. "Sir?"

"What?" Miller walked around the table and right into the officer's face. "Can't you get even a sense that I might be in the middle of something here?"

"Sorry sir, it's just . . ."

"What, it's just what?" Miller asked impatiently.

"Central just told us that they got a call tipping them off about the location of a body. Upstate."

"And?" the captain asked.

The officer had no choice but to respond in front of Nestor. "The tip-off said the body was put there by Danno Garland. Sir."

The captain was suddenly quiet. So was Nestor.

"Do you know anything about this?" Captain Miller asked Nestor. Nestor shook his head.

"What do you want to do?" the officer at the door sheepishly asked his superior.

There was no response. So the officer tried a little prodding. "If you think we have something on this guy, we should move now."

Nestor couldn't believe what he was hearing. How did this get by him? He knew Danno wasn't the killing kind. He figured it must have been something to do with the murder of his wife. "This tip-off. Is it credible?" Nestor asked.

"Central says the caller left dates, times, places. It was someone who knew what they were talking about."

Nestor knew Miller was watching his reaction. He couldn't let it be seen that the new information affected him in any way.

"What do you want to do, sir?" the waiting officer asked.

Captain Miller weighed up everything he had before answering. There was no other answer he could give. "Tell Central there is an ongoing investigation here and that we'll handle this."

Nestor jumped up from his seat.

"But not you," the captain said to Nestor. "You're staying here with me."

"And Danno Garland?" the officer asked.

"Find him. But hold position. If there is something to this I want it done right. And above board. I don't want anyone doing anything without my say-so."

The officer left the doorway to relay the captain's orders. Nestor tried to cover his disappointment and frustration but did a bad job.

"Enough of the bullshit. You're going to stay here and tell me everything you know about this man," the captain warned.

Ricky's heart thumped in his chest as he sped up way more than he was comfortable with. He tore along the narrowing Seven Lakes Drive. On either side of him were rust-colored trees and giant boulders stubbornly protruding from the ground. Miles and miles of forest and trail—a perfect place to hide a body.

Unless someone ratted you out.

Ricky wasn't even sure if Mickey Jack Crisp had done what he asked him to do, but he had to find out. There was Danno and his protection—Ricky always, always protected the boss—but there was also Ricky and his own protection. If Proctor King's body showed up, Danno wasn't the only one who would have to answer some difficult questions. Ricky thought of Ginny, alone. He thought of his life taken from him. All because of the actions of another man. He raged at himself for being so selfish. He knew in his business, the business came first. All the players were expendable.

In his rearview mirror, Ricky saw a sight that stopped his breath: the impatient flicker of red and blue lights approaching him through the thick upstate fog. Otherwise, the road was long and empty. Had Tanner sold him out already? He rushed through the contents of his car in his mind. Was there anything? Anything at all that they could pick up on? What about those new tests he saw on TV that they could do now? Tests that picked up on stuff you couldn't even see.

Ricky released his foot slightly from the gas and looked for any turning opportunity, left or right. The siren grew louder and more intimidating as the green and black Plymouth Fury grew visible through the murk. Quickly they were on him, aggressively pulling closer to his car and backing off.

What the fuck?

Ricky slowed down and watched as the squad car overtook him and continued at full speed along the narrow road. He slid to a relieved stop and watched his greatest fear melt into the distance ahead of him. Ricky had a quick laugh of pure relief. Until it hit him.

They weren't looking for him. Yet. But they were heading where he was heading.

Ricky locked his steering wheel and screeched 180 degrees to point his car back toward the city. He didn't know how to do any more to cover up what Danno had done. What he did know was that it was time to run from it.

Danno felt he could breathe. In his own kitchen, he felt a sense of natural sadness and remorse. He didn't know why, but he felt he could let down his guard somewhat around Lenny Long. Out of the corner of his eye, he watched his old driver dart around his cabinets and refrigerator.

"There's only eggs, boss," Lenny said.

Lenny could see that there was obviously something wrong with Danno. He just didn't know how to ask. The timing seemed all wrong.

"What's your plan?" Danno asked.

Lenny felt like he was caught. Like Danno knew more than he should know as to why Lenny was really there.

"Plan?" Lenny asked.

"In Vegas," Danno said. "What are you going to do for money?"

Lenny was relieved that Danno's question didn't mean what Lenny thought it meant.

"I'm still working on the money thing, boss."

Danno liked that Lenny still called him boss. That word made Danno feel something close to responsible for Lenny. Like there was a bond between them. Maybe even a friendship. When Lenny first came to Danno he was a mark. He didn't know shit about how the professional wrestling business truly worked. But now Danno saw him differently. He saw that Lenny had a goodness in him that was lacking in all corners of the business. Lenny loved wrestling. There were very few in the business who could say that. Danno had loved it once too. He had been in awe of it when his father was boss. He wasn't allowed inside, though. His father never seemed to want Danno anywhere near wrestling. Now Danno could see why.

Lenny twirled the pan in his hand in a move of confidence—and dropped it on the floor. The clang of it nearly made Danno jump out the window with fright.

"What the fuck . . . ?"

"Sorry," Lenny said. He picked up the pan, wiped it with his shirt and laid it gently on the stove.

It was getting overcast and cold outside. The open windows let some new life into the house, but with it came a cold nip.

"Can you take me somewhere, Lenny?" Danno asked.

"Drive you?"

"Yeah."

Lenny smiled. It had only been a little while, but it felt like old times. "It would be my pleasure, boss."

Danno stood. "We'll have something when we get back."

Lenny definitely knew there was something really wrong. He never heard Danno turning down food before.

"Okay," Lenny said.

Danno leaned over to close the top of the window and saw a child wandering around outside.

What the fuck?

"Do you see that?" Danno asked.

"See what?" Lenny replied as he looked out the window and saw his son. "He's mine."

"Yours?"

"It's my boy," Lenny said. "Or one of them. I told them both to wait outside." Lenny opened the door and Luke was standing there with his little brother now in his arms. Both children looked scared and freezing.

"I played Mommy's song in the car for as long as I could," Luke said to his father. "But he still wanted to know where you were."

"Come in, come in," Danno said to the young boys.

Luke waited for his father's okay before moving. Lenny motioned him into the house with a flick of his head. "I just didn't want them making your house sticky," Lenny said to Danno.

"Not at all," Danno opened the door wider than Lenny had, and the two boys entered. They were shaking, half from the cold and half from being left outside in the dark on their own.

"Does he stand?" Danno asked Luke of his little brother in his arms.

Luke was too scared to answer. He just gently placed his little brother beside him and helped his wobbly little body stand up straight.

"Answer the man," Lenny said to Luke.

"He . . . falls a lot but he's getting better," Luke shyly said to Danno.

Danno took a fifty out of his pocket and gave it to Luke. "Are they coming with us?" Danno asked.

"I'm here without Bree. Just a flying visit."

"How about your mother?" Danno wondered.

"She and my father are gone . . ." Lenny didn't want to bore Danno with the details. "She's not there either. We're just spending a night or two in her place and then heading back to Vegas."

"You really got out here?" Danno asked.

Lenny nodded. "Where are we going?" he asked.

This was not a job executed with precision. There were several sets of tire marks that wore a perfect pathway to a mound of freshly turned soil. It was messy; the work of amateurs or someone who didn't expect anyone sniffing around. The longer-serving members of the department could hardly believe their luck. The tip-off was perfect in its placement of the grave. The snitch brought them right to the mark and they were carefully treading all around it, so as not to fuck anything up.

"Precision," shouted one officer as they got out of their cars. "We do this one slowly, and by the book."

They began to survey the area and more than one of the cops commented on it being a beautiful place to be buried. On the side of Bear Mountain, in a forest clearing with the Hudson in view. If you had to be executed and buried, this was the place.

A couple of uniforms cordoned off the area while another pair got suited up for the dig. By the sloppiness of the site, they were expecting it to be a shallow grave and a short day.

"Right, take it slow," came the order as the rain began to fall again. "Captain wants this one to be meticulous."

With just the first shovelful of dirt they exposed a corner of black plastic. Just as it was described to them.

"Bingo."

"Already?"

"Yep."

Lenny took it easy in his father's Ambassador. On the way to Danno's house he had put the convertible top down to impress his sons but couldn't get it back in place. Danno sat in the passenger seat with Luke sitting awkwardly on his lap. There were only two seats so James Henry was on the floor of the car between Danno's feet, bawling loudly, tears streaming down his face.

"It's okay," Luke leaned down and whispered to his little brother.

"I think he shit himself," Danno said of James Henry.

All in all, it was a lovely ride.

Lenny opened the trunk and took out his travel bag and removed a diaper and a towel from it. He also checked to make sure the money he had found in his hotel room was still at the bottom of the bag. Lenny was just waiting for the right time to give Danno back his money, collect his wife's rings, and head on back to Vegas before Bree knew he was gone. He could see that there had been a major change in Danno since he left New York less than a week ago. Lenny just didn't know what was wrong.

Danno and Lenny sat on the freshly painted bench in the cemetery. Lenny had the bag of money between his feet. The two boys charged around the grass in front of the bench. Both kids had bags of candy clasped in their hands. It was getting colder as the night settled in, but sugar and horseplay kept the children warm enough.

Lenny sat in shock as he listened to Danno talk about what had happened in Texas. "They only found her the next day when she didn't answer her wakeup call. I flew down there but they wouldn't let me take her home. Said they needed to wait for someone to sign off on something. After all of our time together and I had to wait for someone else's permission to take my wife home."

"Why?" Lenny asked, as he genuinely tried to think of a reason why anyone would harm such a lady.

Danno didn't hesitate to answer. "Because I tried to outthink everyone. I let her go to Texas. I let her get involved in this fucking business. And it . . ."

Danno took out the envelope Nestor gave him. "And that's what I have left."

Lenny wanted to do something or say something more substantial, but he had no idea how to fill the pause. He watched his former boss and idol wither before his eyes. Listening to Danno's story of what happened to Annie reminded Lenny just how much he loved his own wife. And how much he missed her. He thought about how he'd love to stay but he just wanted to be wherever she was. New York, Nevada—it didn't matter.

Danno turned to Lenny with a crazed look in his eye. "Curt left me a message before . . . but I don't know what he meant," Danno said. "The bag wasn't light. The money was right, wasn't it?"

Danno could see his sudden intensity was making Lenny nervous. He stopped himself.

"Wasn't it, Lenny?" Danno asked calmly.

Lenny stuttered out a response. "What?"

"On the message, he said something about the money was light."

Danno knew the rucksack came from Lenny's place. Lenny Long, he thought, the one person in the business who wouldn't fuck him over.

Lenny managed to muster up a slight shake of his head. "That's not true. The money was right."

If Danno had looked around he would have seen clearly that Lenny was lying. All the pieces started to form in Lenny's mind: the horror of what happened, and his place in it. It made him dizzy and disoriented.

"Well, then she was a stupid fucking bitch," Danno said out of nowhere.

Lenny nervously stood up and Danno immediately reined himself back in. "The kids . . . I'm sorry," Danno said.

"No, no. It's cool," Lenny replied. He could see Danno pore over all the details in his head.

"I just don't know what the fuck happened," Danno said.

With his foot, Lenny slid the bag of money under the bench, out of sight.

"I need to be out there," Nestor said.

"Why?" the captain asked. "What's your fascination with this man?"

They were both sitting now. The room was filled with Captain Miller's smoke. Nestor was now more openly anxious about what was happening outside the building because he had no idea what was going on.

"Why do *you* need to be out there?" Miller asked.

Nestor said, "Do you have any idea how long I've been working for this collar?"

"And still you let him go last night?" Miller asked.

"I need him outside. If we had brought him in last night, how long do you think we would have had him for? On what charge?"

The captain laughed. "So you're running this case now?"

Nestor was too hot. He slid off his jacket and hung it on the back of his seat. It gave him time to think. To try to say the right thing. "We need him outside now because he's making mistakes," Nestor said. "You know this is like a fucking equinox or something, Captain, right? These men don't surface that often. And we have the boss of the whole fucking thing, running around out there with no one to rein him back in."

"What are you saying, detective?" Miller took another long pull from his cigarette and tapped the ash onto the floor.

Nestor knew that stonewalling was wasting his time. He needed to get going. He needed to get a position on Danno. "I've been following Danno Garland on and off for a while," Nestor said.

"And?"

"And nothing. I have absolutely nothing. That's my point. The mistakes that are happening now are a one-off deal."

"And his lawyer? Troy Bartlett?"

Nestor paused a second. He didn't want to have to say any more, but he had to. "I have him. I've been shifting him around for the last few days."

Captain Miller nodded with a knowing smile. "Why?"

"Because I was trying to isolate Danno. Disorient him. Anytime we pick up one of his guys for anything, this fucking guy Bartlett swoops into the picture and has them released within a couple of hours. Danno isn't as strong without someone like him in his ear."

Now the picture was forming for the captain. "Why all the running around behind my back?" he asked.

"Why?"

"Yeah, fucking why. You heard me."

Nestor wondered just how much Miller could handle. How much truth he really wanted to hear. He decided to find out. "Because I don't know you," Nestor began. "But we both know why you were sent here. We both know what the last guy in your position was. We know what most of the guys who work here are. Dirty. Dirty fucking cops."

"And you're not?" Miller asked.

Nestor shook his head and meant it. "I want to get this bastard. And I want to nail him on something that's going to stick. But bringing any cases back into this department is stupid. Nothing stays in these walls. Everything leaks. So I kept this one to myself."

"And how are you going to get him? How are you going to nail Danno?" the captain asked.

Nestor replied. "With paper. He has an office on West Forty-Second that's full of everything I need—enough to not only pull Danno down, but to pull them all fucking down."

Miller asked, "Who are you getting that from? How do you know?"

It was Nestor's turn to laugh. "His own fucking lawyer gave us that tip-off. Bartlett says there's records, files, receipts, contracts—the fucking works in that office."

The desk officer knocked on the door again, only this time he didn't wait to be invited in. "Sir, they've found the grave. Just like the tip-off said."

Nestor instinctively stood up.

"Sit," Miller ordered.

Nestor sat down again like a petulant child. He knew his case was being pulled from him and there was nothing he could do about it.

"Keep me informed," the captain said to the officer, who nodded and left.

"You think no one at that scene is crooked? You think Garland won't know in less than an hour what was found out there?" Nestor said.

Miller stared at Nestor.

"Let me go and get Garland," Nestor pleaded. "I can sew this case up."

The captain shook his head.

Nestor was seething. "He's going to pay his way out of this again."

Captain Miller took a long drag from his cigarette before he flicked it at Nestor. "The only fucking one who looks dirty in all of this is you."

Danno apprehensively approached his wife's grave. He walked like a man who was sure she might reject him somehow. He'd never been this close. When she was being buried Danno had stood way back at the trees. He wasn't ready to say goodbye. Not without holding some form of apology. Not without some kind of justice for her. He was taken aback by the starkness of witnessing his own wife's grave. It was too early to be anything other than a mound of dirt waiting for a headstone. But she was under there. He could see her in his head. Haunting him. Questioning him. Reaching out for him when she was on the floor and the last gasps of life were leaving her body.

Where was he? Where was Danno when she needed him?

Back in the cemetery parking lot, Lenny was in the car with his boys. Little James Henry was asleep in the dark on the passenger seat. He had Danno's coat over him and the tape of Bree singing playing softly in the background. Luke sat on his father's lap and rested his head on his chest. Lenny was telling his son a story with his mouth, but his mind was churning everything that had happened.

"And then the giant walked across the ring and punched me right in the face. His hand was the size of a typewriter. And I went down like a ton of bricks in the cage," Lenny said.

A movement in the side view mirror caught Lenny's attention. He noticed a cop flanking the car. And then another behind him. Lenny put his finger to his lips as he covered his son's mouth with his hand.

"Open," one cop whispered as he shone his flashlight through the window.

Lenny quickly rolled down his window. The cop studied the occupants of the car. Two children and a man who looked nothing like who they were looking for.

"Move along. Now," he said to Lenny.

"Okay," Lenny replied as he quickly started his car.

He counted ten more cops walking toward the cemetery as he left.

At the crime scene, the rainwater was beginning to pool in various pockets of the plastic. Two white-suited forensic officers were ready to expose the body just as soon as the photographer was ready and in place.

In the station, the captain and Nestor waited as the desk officer walked back and forth outside their open door with a large, gray, brick-like walkie-talkie in his hand.

"They're ready, sir," the officer informed his captain. "We also have a team waiting to arrest Garland."

Captain Miller gave the tense, silent order with a nod of his head. "Let's do both at the same time."

"I don't know what to do," Danno said at Annie's grave. "I want to follow you but I don't have the balls to do it. I wanted to kill the man who put you here but I didn't get to him in time. I fucking can't do anything to make this better and it's tearing me all up." Danno finally began to mourn. His tears rolled down his face and his body began to shiver as he took in the reality of life without her. He fell, one weak knee at a time, into the dirt and sobbed uncontrollably.

"There's nothing here for me anymore. I don't care about the money, or the business. I was just trying to show you that I'm a man. That I could get you everything that I thought a woman like you should have. I took over for you. I kept imagining you thinking of him. Comparing me and what I didn't have. I did your thinking for you. And it ended up poisoning me. The wondering and the guessing. I took over the business for you. So you'd love me more back. So you'd stop looking outside what we had to make yourself happy. I wish I talked to you more. I should have stepped in and told you you were my wife and I thought the world of you. I should have handled you better. And laughed with you more. I did you wrong when you were here with me. And I couldn't even make it right when you were gone. But I'm getting my due now. Here, on my own. I can understand you now. And it's too late." Danno's tears turned to anger. "If

I could have just made him feel something like this . . . if I could just have got my fucking hands on him."

Danno roared with frustration and fury.

The freshly turned soil was now piled atop itself beside the newly excavated grave, and the black plastic sheet was exposed enough to lift it fully.

The photographer was shielded from the rain. "Ready," he said as he stood with his camera primed.

"Do it," the field detective said as he looked around to make sure everything was set.

The line of cops at the cemetery walls moved quietly and quickly through the gate. They took up a new, covert position just inside and waited for their next order.

"Well?" Captain Miller asked impatiently from the interview room. "Do we know if it's one of Garland's associates?"

"No word, sir," the desk officer replied as he waited for a voice on his walkie-talkie.

"We find a body, we can bring him down," Miller said to Nestor. "We'll make everything stick."

The desk officer's walkie-talkie crackled to life. "Go. Over."

"It's empty. Repeat, the grave is empty. There's nothing in there. Over."

"It's empty?" Nestor asked. "Is that what they said?"

Miller stood. "Do not approach Danno Garland."

The desk officer ran back to his position to orchestrate the stand down immediately.

"You going to put me out there now?" Nestor asked. "'Cause this department are experts at wasting everyone's fucking time and I'm the only shot you have at getting this guy."

CHAPTER EIGHTEEN

Ricky pulled up outside his apartment and hurriedly got out of his car. He fumbled for his keys as he approached his apartment door. He didn't know what was happening or what Tanner Blackwell had told the cops.

"Ricky?" Nestor called as he crossed the street.

Ricky contemplated running, but stopped instead.

"You got a minute, man?" Nestor asked.

Ricky slowly turned. He looked around for other cops but didn't see anything out of the ordinary. He didn't even know if Nestor was a cop. But he had a strong feeling that he was.

"Can I come up?" Nestor asked as he came closer.

"Who are you?" Ricky asked.

"You don't remember me?" Nestor asked.

"No."

Nestor confirmed Ricky's suspicion about him by pulling out his badge and flashing it.

"A few years ago I showed up to Danno's old house. His car was burned to the ground. You took out a wedge of money and left it on the windowsill. For the window guys, you said."

Ricky knew the face in front of him now.

Nestor continued, "I picked up your money from the windowsill that day and made a decision. I wanted to find out why a person would pay the cops not to solve a crime against them."

Ricky remembered that Nestor was the cop that had left the money on the windowsill. It was so unusual for a cop to not take a bribe, it stuck with him. "And what do you want?"

Nestor leaned against Ricky's parked car. It was cold in the shadow of the building. Ricky didn't notice.

"Something is going down with all your people. There's things leaking out that are making my people very interested in you."

Ricky could hardly keep his body from shaking.

Nestor said quietly, "Before the day is out, they're going to get Danno. No doubt." Nestor blew into his hands and rubbed them together. "All everyone downtown is wondering now is—who else is going down with him? How fucking big is that chain across the country? You know we'll get the evidence to find out."

Nestor could see that Ricky was doing a fine job holding himself together. He needed to push more. "How do you think Ginny is going to do with you on the inside?"

That was the wrong thing to say. "You ever threaten me again," Ricky said, "and I'll—"

"Give up Danno. Come downtown with me. Then, when all this is over, you can move somewhere else and enjoy the last of your queer years on a farm or something."

"Are you here to arrest me?" Ricky asked.

Nestor paused and then shook his head.

Ricky opened his door. "Well then, why don't you get back to your job and find yourself a clean cop to shoot or something?"

"When I get Danno I know you're going to be coming in too. If you give him to me I can look after you—"

Ricky slammed the door in Nestor's face.

Eileen Dean felt bad. For most of her life she had beat herself up about things she really shouldn't have. She was getting on in years and now spent most of her time in Arizona with a man who came and went, which suited her perfectly. She wasn't close to her daughter, who had moved to New York about ten years before.

Eileen blamed herself for that, which was what she always did. She was pretty much at home with the fact that she wasn't maternal. She just didn't have what she just didn't have. She had fed and clothed her daughter and always made sure she was safe. Eileen just didn't do much in the way of affection.

That ate her up too.

She wanted it to be different with him. She wanted to be the grandmother that she saw in her head: the one with the apron on, who was always tending to something delicious in the oven.

Eileen had come into a little money when she sold her house, so now was the time. She invited her daughter and grandson to Disneyland. After all, that was where happy families went. At least in Eileen's head.

Eileen's daughter declined but Eileen was allowed to take her grandson with her.

What a fucking mistake that was.

Eileen could hardly contain how much she hated him as they walked back to her car. She had just spent five days looking after the whiniest little prick she had ever laid eyes on.

"That's too high, Nana."

"It's too hot."

"I've got a sore tummy."

"I miss my momma."

"When are we going?"

"I don't like burgers."

"That mouse is scary."

He was fifteen years old.

Eileen was used to her own space. She thought she could manage. She couldn't. She was terrified that if he opened his mouth once more she might punch him in his tiny, spotty face.

She tried to spend her guilt away, but all that did was leave her drag all that guilt with her through the massive parking lot. Half-deflated balloons, toys, candy, hats, buttons, and two huge suitcases.

She watched with disdain as her grandson walked with trepidation across the noisy parking lot. The only time he forgot where he was was when he caught a glimpse of himself in a car window.

"Nana. Where is your car?"

"We're nearly there," she answered.

"Where is it, Nana?"

Even the way he called her "Nana" she found weird and a little creepy.

"I don't know what it's called. It's beside the brown car straight ahead."

The grandson took off into a floppy run that was embarrassing to even look at. He came up to the back of Eileen's rental car and stubbed his sandaled toe, which propelled him face first into the trunk.

"Nana," he squealed.

Eileen used one of the bags to cover her face while she laughed as the image of him falling played over in her mind.

"Coming," she said between convulsions. She tried to hurry with all her branded, plastic, and sugared cargo. "Coming."

Eileen knelt down beside him. "Did you have an accident?"

"You saw it," he answered back.

"No, an accident."

Eileen sniffed the air and her stomach turned at the smell wafting around.

"No," the grandson answered very matter-of-factly.

"Smells like you did," she said as she stood.

Then he began to smell it too. It was strong and pungent. And close. Eileen seemed to know instinctively that there was something wrong. The scent brought her to the brown Plymouth parked beside her. She cupped the windows and looked in.

"What is it, Nana?" he asked.

She shushed him and continued her inspection of the car. His voice and the way he called her "Nana" was making her stomach worse.

She noticed inside the car was messy and there was muck on the floor, but nothing to account for the type of stifling odor around them.

"It's coming from the trunk," he said, still sitting on the ground.

Ricky had known somewhere in the back of his head that it was going to end like this. Danno just wouldn't give up, and that put them all at risk. The way the business was set up was that if anyone from outside got access, then it was only a matter of time before the whole business went down. Especially if that *someone* was the cops.

The wrestling business's web-like setup was what made them so strong and—now that they were breached—it was that web-like setup that could pull them all down together.

Ricky Plick didn't have the time or the knowledge to hide what needed to be hidden. He wasn't familiar enough with the office to know what was legit and what should never be found.

He just knew that somewhere in this office there was a lot of stuff that should never be seen by anyone outside the business. Which was why he stood at the door of Danno's office on West Forty-Second with a gas can and a pocket full of matches.

He rushed to the floor of the New York Booking Agency knowing that this office made Danno who he was. This room laid claim to the territories and the wrestlers. In their world, the contents of this office made Danno the boss. Outside of their world, it made them all criminals, thieves, and match-fixers. The New York Booking Agency was the center of the whole operation that could end it all for everyone, across the Americas. Ricky couldn't stand by and let that happen.

He poured out the gas along the floor and doused the filing cabinets with it. He splashed it liberally left and right as he shimmied backwards toward the door. He knew that the match he struck meant that they couldn't build a case against Danno based on his own records. He also knew this meant that if Danno couldn't lay claim to his territories and his champion, then anyone could. The fire would throw the red meat of a vulnerable business to the men who had wanted it all along. But what else could he do with the cops moving in so fast?

The only thing Ricky brought with him were the contents of Danno's safe. He figured that would get him and Ginny out of the way for a while. Just till all of this settled down into whatever shape it was to take next.

With a strike of his match Ricky both saved and ruined Danno Garland.

The call came in and sent a concentrated pulse through Captain Miller. He couldn't stick to a fast walk. He burst into a sprint along the corridor. "What the fuck is going on?" he shouted to no one in particular.

All the initial information pointed to it being Proctor King in the trunk of the brown Plymouth. The height, age, and skin color matched. Danno had been picked up in that same airport just the night before. And then released again by Nestor Chapman.

All Captain Miller knew was the snitch on the phone was good. The tip-off was reliable. They now had a body. They could build a serious case. They just needed Danno. Miller just had to make sure one person didn't step in and fuck it all up—on purpose or not. "Chapman. Get me Nestor Chapman," he shouted to anyone who passed him. "I don't want him anywhere near Danno Garland."

"He's not here, sir," a passing officer replied.

"Fucking find him."

CHAPTER NINETEEN

There was a general sense of panic in Joe Lapine's hotel room. The wrestling world was in chaos. All the other bosses had gathered and they wanted answers from their chairman. There were threats thrown and new lines being drawn. There was finger pointing and jostling for position. Joe was thinking, trying to make sense of the situation Danno had put them in.

Tanner Blackwell was all out of thoughts. "Enough," he finally said as he rose from his seat.

The room collectively calmed down and waited. It wasn't just the remaining bosses in the Americas present—it was the bosses from across the globe. They had arrived for Annie Garland's funeral and found themselves caught up in a meltdown.

"Danno Garland is going to be pulled today for the murder of Proctor King. I have it from someone on the inside," Tanner told the gathering. "He'll be collared for the Senator Tenenbaum attack too."

Tanner's revelation sparked up the tension and confusion in the room again.

"Quiet," Tanner said. He was clearly delighted with what he had to say next. "Now I know all of you are wondering what the fuck is going on and what's going to happen to us. But this is the best of a fucked-up situation, folks. We got a boss who kept pushing and pushing until something gave way. We all know that New York has been a mess since he took over. He's made his money and he could have passed the belt on to you or me like a gentleman. Instead he decides to do this and threatens all our livelihoods." Tanner had the room by the balls. He was feeling it now. "Now I heard you all talking about wanting to get the next plane out of here. Well, you go ahead and do that. I'm going to stay here and do what needs to be done. What my dear mama used to call *pickin' the chicken.*"

Tanner stopped his performance to light a cigar and take in the confusion of the room. They were all waiting on him now to make sense of a horrible situation. "When Danno goes away, he's going to take all these problems we're having with him. But." Tanner paused. "He's also going to leave behind his treasure trove of goodies. He's got no one. It's not like he's leaving all his territories to anyone. Who has the fat fuck got?" Tanner asked with a laugh. "So where are his assets going to go?"

Joe had finally heard enough. "All right," he said from his sitting position. "It's time to retreat. There's no one in this room wants any part of this. Go back to your own territories and survive however you can until this all goes away." Joe stood up and opened his hotel room door for them all to leave. "We need to go back to what we were. Back underground."

Crystal Montrose lay in a pool of blood in her brother's house. Her husband didn't get the money. Her brother could do nothing to stop it. Her daughter ran into the darkness behind the house.

Danno slipped into the cold arms of the suit that had laid on his bed. He was clean-shaven and wearing his best shoes. He felt ready to move on. He noticed the reflection of the envelope that Nestor had given him sitting on the nightstand behind him.

His wife was gone. His business meant nothing to him anymore. He was old and had no one.

He took his waiting gun and jammed the barrel into his temple to see how far he would let himself go. His heart began to thump and his contorted face in the mirror startled him. He began to fear just how easily his reflection was changing. No sleep, no wife, no revenge, and no way to stop this choking pain. Danno sucked in angry breaths through his teeth and let them escape again, projecting spit on his lips. His body was petrified because his conscience held the gun. And Danno Garland's conscience was in an angry, bitter, and deluded place. It was gnawing at him, taunting him for being less than a man. For not being able to protect his wife and not even being able to avenge her death.

He peeled back the hammer and remembered the seconds before he killed Proctor in the clearing. It was the same. It felt the same. He felt the same. His mind taunted him that he should have walked away and let Annie have the life that she wanted to live. Instead he stayed and forced her to be with him. How repulsed she must have been by him. How many times she must have laughed with Shane Montrose about him.

Danno moved the barrel from his temple to his mouth and clenched his teeth down hard. His trigger finger was paralyzed. He wanted something to remember her by.

He shook the gun free from his hand and walked over beside his bed. He rested on his knees and opened Nestor's envelope with a slice of his finger. He tilted it and an earring fell out onto a crease in the bedclothes. Danno thought it might have been from a pair he bought her one year for her birthday.

He wished he could remember for sure. Remembering would have helped him believe that he was a better husband. That he noticed the little things and treasured his time with her. He emptied the envelope. Inside there were a couple of rings, a receipt, and a wrapped, hard-boiled sweet that made Danno cry.

It was for her flight. To help pop her ears. That he knew. That was his wife and something she would do. He couldn't contain himself as he remembered buying her the sweets and a magazine in the airport before she left.

And there was a scrap of paper.

Danno didn't recognize the rings, but that wasn't unusual. Annie had a little chest of jewelry that her mother left her when she died.

But the scrap of paper?

It read:

I'M SORRY BOSS. I DON'T HAVE ALL THE MONEY. I WILL PAY YOU BACK. I PROMISE. I'M SORRY. LENNY.

Lenny?

Danno needed a second to think. To cobble together what was happening. *I don't have all the money? I will pay you back?*

Danno wiped his eyes and slowly made his way to his feet, deep in thought.

Captain Miller stopped at the top of Danno's drive and scouted the large house at the end of the drive. He could see no lights or signs of life, but decided to drive down slowly just in case.

"Wait here," he radioed to the two other patrol cars behind him.

"The money was fucking light," Danno roared. "She didn't have the fucking money."

He was turning over his kitchen with rage. He flipped his table and smashed the answering machine against his refrigerator. He pulled his toaster onto the floor before twisting and yanking an open cabinet door off its hinges. He collapsed with his heart pounding too fast. He struggled to catch his breath. Lenny had left him at the cemetery. *Was he in on my wife being murdered? Did he help? Did he give information? Did he steal money that ended up getting my wife killed?*

Danno calmly and sharply snapped. He knew Lenny had lied to him about the money being light. Lenny Long had betrayed him. And his wife.

Lenny was the man he had been looking for all along.

Captain Miller parked his car and cautiously walked the steps to Danno's house. He looked back to make sure the patrol cars had obeyed him.

"Danno?" he shouted at the darkened house. "Danno, this is Captain Matthew Miller of the New York Police Department."

Miller banged the front door. "NYPD."

Danno stood in his fully lit kitchen with the back door open. He had on his best suit and his pocket was heavy with his gun. He waited for Miller to come around. To see him.

"Danno?" Miller shouted as he walked into the light.

"Yeah?" Danno replied.

Captain Miller stopped in the doorway and looked around at the overturned kitchen. "You doing all right in here?" he asked.

Danno slowly nodded.

"I was truly sorry to hear about Annie, Danno," Miller said. "But you're not going to last another night on the outside. Your guys are willing to rat you out. They have Proctor's body. It's not good."

Danno didn't answer. He didn't even look like he cared all that much.

Miller continued, "I'm sorry to tell you that, but I just thought you should hear it from me. Out of respect to your old man."

Danno cleared his throat. "There's money in the barn, third bale down from the door. On the right. Ten grand or more," he said.

Miller turned in the doorway. "You've got an hour to get out of here. Trust me, a man like you wouldn't do well inside."

"I don't plan on going to prison," Danno replied.

Miller took one last look before he left.

Danno took his gun from his pocket, pushed out the cylinder, and saw one bullet waiting.

It was the bullet that had Danno Garland's name on it from the start.

CHAPTER TWENTY

Nestor and Katy Spence sat silently in Nestor's car, parked on the side of a darkened road. They both watched in silence as Captain Miller's car pulled out of Danno's driveway and was followed by two other patrol cars.

Miller had his radio to his mouth as he passed them.

"What's going on?" Katy asked Nestor.

"Keep your head down," Nestor said as he crouched.

The cars were moving the opposite way but he didn't want to take any chances. Nestor waited in silence until he was sure they were gone.

"What are we going to do?" she asked.

"I'm going to drop you off somewhere. I appreciate the car but . . ."

He could tell she was not happy. Nestor leaned into Katy and kissed her gently. "You've done great work on this case," he said. "I know how nervous you were approaching Danno. But you got him to act. That was you."

Katy said, "I'm not going home. I want to know exactly what you're doing here."

Nestor took a second to ask himself how much he trusted this woman. "There's something about the captain. I don't know, before you say anything. Just something."

He waited for a big reaction. A big rebuttal. There was none. "Okay," Katy said simply. "What's your plan?"

Nestor turned on the ignition. "I don't really have one," he said as he pulled slowly into the road. "I just want to finish this." he said as he switched on his lights.

They drove down the quiet road a little way before noticing a car stopped on the side of the road. As they drove past, Katy's neck swiveled. "Wasn't that . . . ?"

"What?" Nestor asked.

Katy turned to look out the back window as Nestor drove. The parked car's passenger door closed. "That was Danno Garland that got into that car."

Nestor tried in vain to see through his rearview mirror. "What?"

"Yeah. I'm sure it was him. He must have come out onto the road through the field next to his house."

"Are you *sure* sure?" Nestor asked.

"Yeah. One hundred percent. He's in the car behind us."

Nestor looked back and saw the headlights of the car behind him appear around the bend. "We need to pull in somewhere and get behind him."

In the car behind, Danno sat in the passenger seat. He didn't want to run the risk of taking a car of his own to Lenny's mother's house, so he waited by the traffic lights near his house and walked out in front of a slow-moving car with a handful of cash.

Danno had been to Lenny's parents' house once before. It was time he visited again.

Lenny watched his boys settle down on the couch. He knew he should probably go, but they looked so comfortable. And Danno didn't know. Not that Lenny could tell, anyway. He just didn't want to go back to Bree without her rings. Lenny gave them away and he wanted to get them back.

But he didn't know how to do that without telling Danno what had happened.

Nestor and Katy kept their distance and followed Danno's car into a small, quiet, working-class street on Long Island.

"I know you have your doubts," Katy said. "But I thought Captain Miller told you all to contact him before . . ."

"I'm just looking," Nestor said.

Katy wasn't comfortable. "I think we should . . ."

Danno's car slowed down as he tried to see which house was Lenny's parents' house. The car stopped suddenly in the middle of the street.

"We're not doing anything wrong," Nestor reminded her as he pulled into a nice dark spot. "When we identify the passenger as Danno Garland, we'll call it in. Okay?"

Lenny saw car lights drift down his parents' street. Normally such a thing wouldn't even catch his attention, but this evening had him twitchy. He walked to the window and saw Danno getting out of a car he didn't recognize.

"Quick," Lenny said to his kids. "Up, up."

Luke sat up and rubbed his eyes. Lenny looked around for a quick, safe place. Just in case.

"Go and hide," he told Luke as he handed him his little brother.

"What's happening?" Luke asked.

Danno knocked on the door. "Lenny?" His voice wasn't angry and his knock was light enough. But Lenny still wasn't sure.

"Go now," he said to his oldest son.

Luke got the message. He ran for the kitchen, pulling his brother along behind him.

"Don't make any noise," Lenny warned him.

Danno knocked again. "Lenny."

Lenny made sure his boys were in the other room before he walked toward the door. He wasn't a religious man, but Lenny said a little prayer before he turned the doorknob.

Nestor and Katy watched Lenny let Danno into the house. It seemed calm and reasonable. Nestor was struggling with the politics of being there, with a rookie, without notifying anyone else from his precinct.

"What do you want to do?" Katy asked.

"Fuck."

"What?"

"You're right," Nestor admitted. "It's not worth it."

"What?"

"Call it in."

Katy looked around for a pay phone. She was willing to knock on doors and show her badge if she had to.

Danno closed the front door with his heel and immediately produced his gun. He put it to Lenny's head.

"What are you doing?" Lenny said. The fright of seeing a gun so close, and seeing Danno's eyes go dead, made Lenny backpedal. He put himself between Danno and his out-of-sight kids.

"You fucking liar," Danno said.

"Wait," Lenny pleaded. "The kids. Wait."

In the kitchen Luke could hear the voice in the other room. He could see that his little brother was getting scared and agitated. He took him gently by the hand and led him out into the garage. He closed the door.

"We have to be quiet," Luke told James Henry as he put his finger to his lips. The dark was scaring the younger boy. He began to cry and call for his dada. Luke didn't know what to do.

"He can't come to you now, James Henry," Luke explained. "They're just playing. Doing a fight for wrestling. That's Daddy's boss. You hear me?"

But little James Henry was tired and his gums were sore. He was in the dark and scared. He cried as he looked for a way out to find his father.

Luke knew he needed to distract his little brother quickly. He looked up at his grandfather's Ambassador car. "Come with me," he said to his kid brother.

"M'am, we need to use your phone please," Katy said as she barreled her way into the house across the street. "It's official police business."

Nestor sat in the car wondering whether or not his captain was dirty. It didn't feel right to stay seated in his car when Danno was only a few hundred feet away from him. Nestor could finish his job and get the collar. He'd be known as the man who got the boss no one could get.

Danno pushed Lenny back into a seated position and aimed the gun at his head. Tears rolled down his face as he saw his one-time driver in front of him. "How could you do that to me, Lenny? How could you steal from me?"

"I—"

"Can't you see what it did to me?" Danno asked.

Lenny put his head in his hands and pleaded with his former boss, "Please. I . . . I . . . didn't know. I . . . I didn't mean to . . ."

"Shut up," Danno shouted as he turned from pain to anger. "Shut your fucking mouth."

Luke could hear the shouting getting louder in the living area. His brother was sobbing on his lap in the passenger seat of his grandfather's treasured car. Luke wanted to make him better. Make him less scared. He leaned over and turned on the ignition. Exhaust fumes filled the small garage as the engine roared to life.

"Do you want to hear Mommy?" Luke asked.

James Henry nodded. His eyes were big and red and full of tears.

Luke pressed play on the eight-track, turned the volume down to nearly nothing, and held his brother closer. He too was scared, but didn't want his little brother to see. As usual, Bree's voice coming through the car speakers instantly settled James Henry. Even Luke got something from hearing his mother singing this time.

Both little boys sat in the dark in the running car.

Danno put his gun down on the table between him and Lenny.

"Take it," Danno said.

Lenny nodded.

"Take it or I will," Danno warned.

Lenny carefully picked up the gun.

"I'm sorry, Danno," Lenny said.

He meant it too. His heart was broken, thinking of what happened to Annie.

"Use it," Danno said.

"What?"

Danno was done. Finished. Heartbroken and worn down. "You use it on me, or I use it on you," he said.

Lenny moved to put the gun right back on the table.

"Lenny," Danno warned through gritted teeth. "There's one bullet and it's getting fired into one of our heads. That I fucking promise you." Danno couldn't take the pain of being alive anymore. "You will fucking know what I feel like."

"Danno . . . please . . ." Lenny was desperately trying to listen for where his sons were.

Danno rose from his seat as he heard the sirens approaching in the distance. He knew he could wait and spend his life in jail, or act and put an end to all of this. "You have ten seconds to pull that trigger. You fucking hear me? You fucking cunt. You have ten fucking seconds to use that gun or I will. I want your family to know that you killed someone. I want you to know what it feels like to put someone in the ground. You thief. You fucking liar. You killed her," Danno shouted.

"I'm not going to do it," Lenny replied.

Danno moved closer. "I have someone who will track down your wife, Lenny. If I'm alive he will spend every day of his life just following her, waiting for me to give him the word to blow her fucking head off."

The sirens were growing louder.

"Stop," Lenny pleaded. "I don't . . . don't . . ."

Lenny could see by Danno's eyes that he was serious.

"Ten . . ."

"I have the money," Lenny pleaded. "It was an accident."

Danno exploded with rage. "You think I want fucking money? I want you to suffer. You fucking understand me now? I bring you in, I look after you. Annie fucking loved you. And you can do this?"

"But it was a mistake," Lenny said as he broke down. "It was—"

Danno grabbed Lenny by the collar and slapped him across the face. He pulled him out of his seat and locked him forehead to forehead. Danno's face was red and contorted with fury. "Do it," Danno ordered.

Danno wasn't going to jail. There was no way.

"Do it," he repeated.

Nestor knocked on the door. "Danno? Police."

Time was running out. The sirens had arrived and Nestor was now pounding on the door outside.

Lenny was shaking with fear.

"You want me to make the call, Lenny? You want me to have your wife murdered like mine was?" Danno threw Lenny back onto the seat and walked for his parents' phone.

"Three . . ." Danno counted.

Danno picked up the receiver and looked back.

"Two . . ."

Lenny stood. "Don't."

Danno dialed a number and waited.

"Danno," Nestor shouted once more before he kicked the door in.

"One . . ." Danno said with a slight smile on his face.

Nestor watched from the broken doorway with his gun raised. He could see Lenny had the gun and was strongly considering using it. "Lenny. Don't. Lenny?" he shouted.

"Hello?" Danno said into the phone. "It's me. Do . . ."

Lenny fired a single shot at Danno's head that killed him instantly. Nestor fired a round that hit Lenny in the chest. The impact lifted him back into the seat. He was alive but choking on his own blood.

"Medic," Nestor shouted as he entered the house with his gun still raised. "We need a medic."

Lenny tried desperately to tell Nestor about his kids but he couldn't speak through the blood that was filling up his mouth.

Five hours before Danno's murder.

"Mr. Bartlett?" Katy asked again. "Who did Danno Garland sign his assets over to?"

Troy knew his own way out of this shit was to tell her. He could see the file in his mind. He took it from the barn where Danno signed it and placed it deep into his own filing cabinet.

Katy tapped the cage to get his attention.

Troy's head shook in amazement at what he was about to say. "He didn't trust his wife for some reason."

"Who did Danno Garland sign his business over to?" Katy asked more pointedly.

Troy looked her dead in the eye. "His driver."